Lethal Inheritance

Cynthia Hickey

To all those who love a good page turner.

Chapter One

Tatym Billings clutched her small overnight suitcase and stepped off the bus in front of Lucy's Diner in Misty Hollow. The rest of her things would be brought to her once they arrived, or so she'd been told.

The scenery on the almost four-hour drive had been gorgeous. Vibrant greens, fields of grain, pastures of cows and horses. Then, the climb up the mountain—breathtaking. Maybe uprooting her life could be a good thing.

She froze on the sidewalk as a pair of police officers ushered two scantily-clad women into squad cars. Her eyes widened as a man with a star pinned to his shirt stood mere feet away from her, barking orders at the onlookers.

"Step aside, ma'am." The same man—she now knew was the sheriff because she read it under the star—motioned her to move. "Maybe have a seat in the diner."

Her stomach growled on cue making the decision for her, especially after seeing a help-wanted sign in the window. With a nod to the sheriff, she headed across the street, pushed open the glass door of the diner, and approached the hostess. "I'd like to apply for the job posted in the window."

"Lucy? Someone wanting the job," the woman called out, then smiled at her. "She'll be right with you."

"Thanks." She took a seat on a padded bench under a large window and set the suitcase at her feet.

Less than a minute later, a middle-aged woman, her hair tied in a messy bun, came through the kitchen door carrying a clipboard and rushed toward Tatym. "You, my dear, are a lifesaver. Fill these out. You can start immediately. Are you hungry?"

The woman didn't even ask for her name. Misty Hollow sure was a strange town. "As a matter of fact, I am." She wrote her name on the top line.

"How do you pronounce your name?" Lucy bent over, peering closer at the paper.

"Tay-tum."

"Nice way to spell it even if it is confusing. Heather, bring this girl the special. On the house. She's one of us now. Oh, and an apron and a name badge. T. A. T. Y. M. Are you over eighteen?"

"I'm twenty-five." Things were moving way too fast.

"Sure don't look like it. What brings you to town, Tatym?" She enunciated each syllable.

"My grandmother passed and left me the Billings cabin and land." She finished filling in the blanks and handed the clipboard back to Lucy.

"Well, that's nice." Her smile now looked forced. "I wish you all the luck with that. Needs some work. Follow me." She led Tatym through the kitchen to a small staff room. "You can eat here and stash your suitcase in that locker. Here's the combination." She scribbled a set of numbers on a napkin. "You do know how to wait tables, don't you?"

"I'll figure it out. I worked as a receptionist for years, so I know people." Her legs gave way at the suddenness of her new life, or maybe the fact she hadn't eaten anything that day. She grabbed the wall.

Lucy patted her on the shoulder. "You'll be fine. I didn't know much about owning a diner when I bought it from Myrtle, the previous owner. Eat up."

"What happened to the girl I'm replacing?"

"See those women being rounded up outside?"

"Yes." She tilted her head.

"Well, turns out she prostituted herself on her off-hours. She's been arrested. You'll be paid every Friday starting next week, and you can keep all your tips. You'll most likely have to clear tables, too."

"That's fine." She stared at the chicken-fried steak, mashed potatoes, and gravy placed in front of her.

"Eat up. All meals are free for my staff. Welcome to Misty Hollow. Oh, and buy a car quick. It's quite a trip up that mountain and back. I've one you can borrow in the meantime. I'll have someone fetch it."

"Thank you." Tatym shook her head. "Is everyone in the town this friendly?"

"Most of us, but murder likes to shadow this town. Especially when a new girl arrives." Lucy cackled and went back to the kitchen.

Why did the woman think her statement funny? Was she even serious?

She gobbled up her food and donned the yellow frilly apron Heather had brought her. They'd spelled her name correctly. With a smile, she headed to wait on customers.

By the end of her shift at six p.m., her back and feet ached. Her overnight suitcase felt as if it weighed twenty pounds more than it did. An older model sedan waited in back of the diner. Tatym punched her grand…*her* address into the phone's GPS and headed to her new home. She gave thanks for the borrowed car. There was no way she could walked the distance. After following a winding, dirt road, she entered a clearing where a log cabin sat overlooking a valley. "Oh, wow."

Tatym scurried from the car to the edge of the clearing. The town of Misty Hollow lay far below her. Mountains rose around her. Grandma had never said how beautiful the place was. Why had her mother never brought her here? Her grandmother always had to visit them.

Tearing her eyes away from the view, she studied her new home. It was missing chinking between the logs. That would need fixing before winter. The roof was lacking a few shingles, and a shutter hung lopsided from a window. Hopefully, the inside was in better condition.

Her foot plunged through the rotted second step. Using a bit more caution, she crossed the porch and pushed the unlocked front door open.

The cabin wasn't large, but it would suit her needs. The main room consisted of living, dining, and kitchen space, everything horribly outdated. Two bedrooms and one bath completed the house. An attic door pulled down from the center of the living room. Despite the dust covering everything, Tatym smiled and closed the attic. Welcome home, she could hear Grandma saying.

~

The bed of his truck full of boxes, Dane James made his way further up the mountain to the Widow Billings' property. As he stopped in front of the cabin, a tiny woman with hair the color of mahogany stepped onto the porch. He hadn't expected Alice's heir to be so young.

"Miss Billings? I'm Dane James. I've brought your things." The place had needed some work when Alice was alive. Now, it definitely did. His grandmother, June Mayfield, hadn't told him how much needed doing.

"Thank you. I wasn't expecting anyone until tomorrow." She rushed toward him, ponytail bobbing and hazel eyes sparkling a greeting.

"I happened to be in town when they were delivered. Your grandmother is my grandmother's best friend, although neither of them got out much." He heaved a box from the truck bed. "Where would you like these?"

"The smallest bedroom, I guess." She took a box.

The tiny woman was stronger than she looked. "Know of anyone I can hire to fix this place up? First the outside, then renovate the inside?"

"I own a construction company, and I'd love to work on this cabin."

"Really?" She cast wide eyes at him. "That would be great."

"I could start tomorrow. Once the truck is unloaded, I'll take a look around and write up an estimate."

"Are you an honest man, Mr. James?"

"Dane, please, and I'd like to think so. My grandmother would tan my hide otherwise." He grinned and entered the cabin. She hadn't been kidding about it needing some work.

This place would be his first big job. After leaving the job as a ranch hand at the Leaning O Ranch, he'd taken a few odd jobs to put his name out there, but they didn't pay enough to get him out of his grandmother's guestroom. Still, it smelled better than the bunkhouse.

After unloading the truck, he took his cell phone from the passenger seat and took photos of the outside of the house from every angle, then the inside. He sneezed as dust flew from Miss Billings' frantic sweeping.

"Sorry." She stopped and waited for him to finish. "I'm Tatym, by the way. Since you'll be working here, you might as well call me by my first name. You'll be here most of the time by yourself. I'm the new waitress at the diner."

"You'll meet everyone in town eventually." He snapped all the photos he needed, then went back out to write up the estimate. When he'd finished, he joined Tatym on the front porch where she rocked in a wicker chair.

"You'll love the view as the sun rises. I strongly suggest you make a point of waking up early enough in the morning. The mist is a sight to see." He handed her the quote. "This doesn't include renovating the inside or the material."

"Five thousand?" She shrugged. "Okay. My grandmother left enough money to fix the place up. We'll talk about the inside once the roof and walls are fixed. I think I'd like a metal roof, please. An insulated one. It'll last longer." She sighed, her eyes panning the valley. "The sunset is gorgeous."

"You should take a look around your property. The entire ten acres is great. Come on, I'll show you."

"Okay." She leaped to her feet. "Might as well while we can still see. I bet it gets dark up here."

"I'll bring motion-detector lights for both the front of the house and the back." He'd tried persuading Alice to let him install them, but she'd complained it would keep her awake with all the critters that roamed around.

"That sounds great."

Dane led her to the shed on the east side of the house. "Here is where Alice's 1982 truck and riding lawn mower are stored. She kept both in tip-top shape." He slid the door open. "There's also gardening tools if you want to put in a garden."

"I do." She ran her hand over the navy-blue Ford. "Now, I won't have to buy a vehicle." She moved to the small window at the back of the garage and pointed toward the woods. "Who is that? Do I have neighbors up here?"

"Not for a few miles." Dane peered over his shoulder at a man slipping into the trees.

~

He thought he'd had plenty of time before the granddaughter showed up. It didn't matter. She wouldn't be there every hour of the day. He'd dig around when she was gone. The sooner he found what he was looking for, the sooner he could build the resort. People would pay big bucks to stay in a cabin this high on the mountain and watch the sun burn off the early morning mist.

With the fishing, hunting, and hiking in the area, it would become a popular tourist place. All he needed was to 'remove' the last Billings family member.

It had been easy enough to get rid of the old woman. Folks thought she'd died of a heart attack, but he knew better. Too much insulin and voilà. Dead. He'd think up some kind of accident for the granddaughter. Something no one would question. He hadn't come to this hick town for any other reason than to collect what was owed him. It didn't matter what it took—he always got what he wanted.

Chapter Two

Early the next morning, cup of coffee in hand, Tatym stood at the edge of her property and stared at a mist so thick she could walk across its surface. Soon droplets of moisture dotted her arms.

As the sun started to rise, she gasped. The rays kissed the mist with orchid and rose tints before burning it away. Tatym didn't care how long she stayed up the night before; she planned on being right here at sunrise every single morning.

Since she had a few hours before her shift started at ten, she set her empty coffee cup on the rail of the front porch and strolled the perimeter of her property. Wildflowers dotted much of the cleared areas. The grass needed cutting, but the colors made it impossible. At least for now. Mowing could wait.

She turned to where she'd seen the man the evening before. Since Dane had said her nearest neighbor was miles away, what was the man doing there? Curiosity over the town's newest arrival? Or something else? Tatym stopped and stared at the freshly dug hole at the edge of the trees. The hole was too neat to have been made by an animal. Why would someone dig up her yard? Further searching showed another hole under a rosebush in bad need of pruning and another under a young magnolia tree.

With a sigh, she headed to the garage and removed a shovel from a hook on the wall. She was working on the third hole by the time Dane arrived to start chinking the holes between the logs of the exterior wall.

"What are you doing?" He cocked his head.

"Filling in holes." She leaned on the shovel. "Any idea why someone would dig holes in my yard?"

He shook his head and avoided her gaze. "No…"

"That doesn't sound like a firm no."

He shrugged. "It's a silly rumor."

"I'm listening." Her brow arched. Nothing was silly if it answered a question.

He cleared his throat. "Just before Alice died, folks started talking about another deed to this land. One that doesn't have the Billings' name. One rumored to be the real deed, so the one your grandmother had was false. Alice never put much stock in rumors."

Another deed? This land had been in her family for almost a hundred years, or so she'd been told. "That doesn't explain the holes. If the rumor is true, I doubt the deed would be buried."

"Why not? When this land was purchased, a lot of people didn't use the bank to keep documents safe."

"Hmm." She finished filling in the hole, then strolled back to the house, Dane at her side. "I'd best get ready for work," she said, leaning the shovel against the house. Might as well leave it out in case she had more holes to fill when she returned home. "Here's my cell phone number if you have any questions while I'm away." Tatym handed him a piece of paper. His number was on the estimate he'd given her.

An hour later, she helped with the late-breakfast-early-lunch crowd at the diner. "Is it this busy all day?" She brushed a stray strand of hair out of her face.

"Yes," Heather answered. "Lucy does it all before the two of us arrive."

"Why not hire an early-shift waitress?" Or two. Tatym was already exhausted after working the diner alone except for the woman responsible for the counter.

"The sign is still in the window." Heather smiled at a couple of elderly men. "Your seats at the counter are available." She lowered her voice to Tatym. "The one in the coveralls, Walt, knows everything there is to know about this town. He's a real character. Has no problem expressing his opinion."

The man might be the best person for Tatym to talk to. Hopefully, she'd find time in her busy day.

Her heart sank as the man ate and left. She'd have to try harder the next day. Or she could let it go. Why waste time on chasing down a rumor?

The sheriff entered the diner, and Heather led him to a table by the front window. Tatym approached his table. "Coffee while you think about your order?"

He glanced up, his gaze landing on her nametag. "You're new in town."

"Yes, sir. Arrived yesterday during all the commotion." She smiled. "I inherited Alice Billings' property. I'm her granddaughter, Tatym."

"Ah, you're the last surviving family member squatting on that land according to some."

Her smile faded. "I have the deed, sir." Sitting in a safety-deposit box in the bank.

"I'm only kidding."

"I heard the rumor started right before my

grandmother died. Do you know who started it?"

"Nope. It just started floating around town. I'll have the four-egg omelet and coffee."

Tatym went to give the chef the sheriff's order. Her mind dwelled on what the sheriff had said. Someone had to have started the rumor. They didn't start themselves. Tatym planned on finding out who would do such a thing.

~

He watched her wait on customers, listened to her conversation with the sheriff, and clenched his hands so hard his nails dug into his skin. It wasn't a rumor; it was the truth. He'd show them all. He'd tried to be nice to the girl at first, then run her off with threats and take the land. But, if the girl was as stubborn as the old woman, she'd suffer the same fate. His eyes narrowed as she approached the kitchen, passed through, and carried the sheriff's meal to him. Then, he raised his coffee cup for a refill.

"Be right there." She rushed to fetch the pot, returning quickly to top off his cup. "Can I bring you anything else?"

He smiled up at the pretty girl. If he were single and younger, he'd try dating and then marry her. The land would then belong to him, and he wouldn't have to resort to unpleasantries. "No, thank you. Two cups are my limit, and I haven't finished my eggs."

"Just holler if you change your mind." She flashed a wider smile, then left to wait on someone else.

Yep, it would be a real shame to hurt her. He tossed a good-sized tip on the table and went to the counter to pay his bill. He'd be back every day to keep an eye on her. Right now, he needed to put his plan to work.

At the first sight of Dane's truck in front of the cabin, he watched the former ranch hand working on the walls. How much work would he be doing for Tatym? Would he be here every day?

This put a kink in his plans. He slapped the steering wheel and backed slowly down the road before Dane could spot him. There'd be questions he had no answers for. He had no reason to be this high on the mountain. Not without someone needing major construction.

What a waste of time. He sped down the mountain, slowing around curves, and headed back to the office. Too much time away would result in more questions. Everything resulted in questions.

~

Dane enjoyed the repetitive act of putting the chinking mortar between the logs. It soothed him, erasing some of the worry about his business surviving. He'd made a steady income working for O'Ryan on the ranch, but he always dreamed of owning his own business.

His grandmother had told him there was no time like the present to take the leap and offered him free rent if he'd stay under her roof and do some minor repairs. Until Tatym hired him, that had been his only work but didn't put cash in his pocket. He hoped she'd find time to write him a check for the deposit. Dane swiped his spreading tool on the bucket of mortar and straightened at the sound of crunching rocks. Glancing over his shoulder, he caught sight of the top of a truck backing away. People often took drives up and around the mountain which reminded him he had motion lights to install and a roof to order.

When Tatym arrived home, he was working on his

laptop he'd set on the hood of his truck. "You're here late." She pulled a check from her pocket.

"Need to order your roof and want you to pick out the color." He turned the laptop so she could see the choices.

"The charcoal grey." She gave a definitive nod. "I brought some meatloaf from the diner. There's plenty if you haven't eaten."

"Thanks, I am hungry." He placed the order and followed her into the house. "I installed the lights today. Larger animals will trigger them, but anything smaller than a cat might not."

Tatym warmed up their meal in the oven. "I'd offer you something to drink other than water or coffee, but I haven't been to the grocery store yet. Did someone pick up Lucy's car?"

"Yeah. About ten this morning, a young man was dropped off. We waved and that was it. Why?"

She chuckled. "I hoped I wouldn't have to figure out how to return the car. Tomorrow night, I'll pick up groceries on my way home. Luckily, I don't need much. I can eat all my meals at the diner, even bring home leftovers. You're welcome to eat whatever tomorrow's is, too, if you're here late enough."

"If my grandmother doesn't need me, I'd be happy to. I don't dare interrupt her evening shows by coming home in the middle of them. If I'm not home by five, I have to wait until eight." He laughed. "I love that woman, but she's set in her ways for sure."

"I'd love to meet her someday."

"She'd love that. Likes to sit and have tea and cookies. Did it every week for the woman who used to clean her house."

"Who does it now?"

"Me." He grinned. "I don't work on Sundays, so I spend that day cleaning and doing repairs around her place."

"Thankfully, the diner is closed so I can put in a late garden." She pulled the leftovers from the oven and divided it onto two plates. "Enjoy. I slaved all day over the stove."

"Ha ha. But, I am a fan of Lucy's chef's cooking—Chef Rawlings."

"By the way, I watched the sun on the mist this morning."

"And?" He cut into his meatloaf.

"The most beautiful thing I've ever seen."

"Didn't you visit as a kid?" He'd never felt this comfortable around a woman before. Never had been able to make small talk or carry on a lengthy conversation. Tatym's open friendliness made it easy.

"Grandma visited us once in a while, sent me birthday cards and money at Christmas, but I don't think she fully forgave my mother for not marrying my father. My mom was in her thirties, wanted a baby, and…had a friend donate, if you know what I mean. That's the story I was told anyway." She ducked her head and concentrated on her food.

He saw through her flippant attitude. The story she'd been given bothered her.

The back motion light turned on.

Something gave a bloodcurdling scream.

Tatym jumped to her feet, knocking her chair to the floor as she fumbled for the flashlight in the center of the table. "What was that?"

"I don't know. Stay here." He glanced around for a

weapon. Nothing but a fire poker. It would have to do. Clutching the iron piece in his hand, he yanked open the back door.

Chapter Three

Tatym chuckled as she climbed out of bed the next morning remembering the shining green eyes reflected in her flashlight beam. The scream had been nothing more than a cougar protesting the presence of humans. Dane had looked incredibly sexy standing in the doorway clutching a fire poker.

But, she had no business thinking of him as anything more than a friend and hired contractor. She'd just arrived in town. Did she really want to form any attachments?

Tatym padded to the bathroom. The motion light outside came on as it had a few times during the night. She shrugged and turned on the shower. In a night or two, she'd grow used to the light and not pay it much attention.

After a long shower, she poured a cup of the coffee waiting for her in the pot, then opened the front door to see the mist. Rain had fallen during the night giving everything that fresh look and smell.

She gasped and stepped back. The cup fell from her hand and shattered on the wooden boards of the porch.

A mutilated possum lay just outside the door. Was this the work of last night's cougar?

Tatym shuddered and retreated a few more steps in order to grab her flashlight and a broom. After cleaning up the glass, she headed for the garage and a shovel.

By the time she'd buried the possum, the sun had already kissed away the mist. She sighed and returned the shovel to the garage. The crunch of tires alerted her to Dane's arrival. Early, too.

"Roof is being delivered today," he said. "Shipment came early. I need to get things ready. Didn't expect you to be up and around, but I'm glad you are."

"I wanted to watch the mist but buried a dead possum instead." She glanced to where the animal's blood stained her porch. "Guess I have some bleaching today before I head to work. You won't bother me. How about some coffee?"

"No, thanks. No time." He flashed a grin and pulled a ladder from the back of his truck.

Tatym went back to pour herself another cup of coffee, this time sitting at the kitchen table. She peered around, making a mental list of renovations and the order in which she wanted them done. Kitchen first.

Footsteps above her drew her attention to the roof, then the clock. She worked an earlier shift today and needed to be on her way. Maybe waking up early every day wasn't such a good idea.

A few minutes later, she climbed into her truck, tossed Dane a wave, and headed down the mountain. A truck filled with slabs of metal roofing blocked the road. Two tires had slid into the ditch causing the flatbed to tilt and spill some of its load. There'd be no getting around for quite a while. A newer model Ford had stopped a few yards in front of the larger vehicle.

Tatym called the diner and explained the situation.

"I'm so sorry."

"We'll manage," Lucy said. "I'll call my niece. She's been wanting a job, but I've put it off because she's unreliable. Guess she can fill in once in a while. Come in when you can."

Tatym hung up, slid out of her truck, and approached the Ford. "I have someone working up the road. Need him to help?"

A middle-aged man in a hard hat turned and smiled. "Sure do. You Miss Billings?"

"I am. That my new roof?"

"It is. A deer ran out in front of my driver and here we are. I'm Frank Grayson, owner of this outfit."

"I'll be back in ten minutes." Hopefully, Dane's truck could pull them out. She had no idea how they'd get a tow truck in position. She turned around and explained the situation to Dane. He scurried down the ladder. "You want to ride with me?"

"No. Once the road is clear, I still need to go to work." She followed him to the scene of the accident and joined him in surveying the damage.

"We'll have to make a couple of trips to the house with the metal in my truck." Dane crossed his arms. "I can't pull that load from the ditch, but once the bed is empty…"

"Got it." Grayson barked orders to start transferring the roofing material to Dane's truck.

Two men, along with Dane, got to work, leaving Tatym leaning against the fender of her truck to watch. This was going to take a while.

"Sorry about the holdup." Grayson approached her.

"An unfortunate accident. Nobody's fault." She smiled in an attempt to reassure him that she understood.

"How are you liking Misty Hollow?"

"So far so good. I found a job on my first day, the cabin came with a truck, and the view is amazing…" She really did love the place. "Once the cabin is fixed up, things will be perfect."

"I agree. That view is amazing." Something flickered in his eyes that seemed to contradict his wide grin.

She tilted her head. "You've been up here?"

"Sure, I have. Your grandmother allowed anyone that wanted to see the view to come up. It's not the only place on the mountain to see the mist, but it is one of the best."

Tatym didn't think she wanted people traipsing around. Especially since she wanted to put in a garden, plant some flowers…not have to worry about leaving things out. "I'm afraid I'm not as accommodating as my grandmother." At least not right away.

~

He'd almost laughed out loud when she'd dropped her cup after spotting the gift he'd left her. There were plenty more gifts planned, and he hoped he'd be lucky enough to see her reaction to them. He'd wanted to install some cameras so he could watch from anywhere, but the roofing-truck accident had paused that idea.

Finding time when James wouldn't be around or would be too busy to notice him wasn't easy. He might have to come under the cover of darkness. Those stupid lights made that more difficult, but he had to find that deed.

Last night he'd reread the letter his grandfather had left him. Unfortunately, it only said the deed existed, not its exact location. Just that the Billings who had built the cabin had buried it. Which he took to mean it wouldn't be in the cabin. What if it had been buried under the cabin?

Under the porch would be a good spot. It sat high enough for a man to crawl under. Digging there without being caught was the trickiest idea yet.

~

After the fifth trip, Dane realized he wouldn't get much of the roof on today. Now, he studied the lopsided vehicle. "If we both pull with our trucks," he told Grayson, "We might be able to pull it free."

"Worth a try. The day is wasting away, and Miss Billings is starting to pace."

Dane glanced her way. Sure enough, she walked up and down the road. There'd be little work for her today.

He grabbed a set of chains from the bed of his truck and hooked them to the front, leaving the side in the ditch for Grayson. His truck was bigger and had more horsepower—something Dane intended to remedy when he had the funds.

His tires spun on the wet dirt road as he pressed the accelerator. The truck's back end swerved. Inch by inch the flatbed started to move. After a few minutes, he realized things weren't going as well as he'd hoped. The flatbed swung toward where Tatym now stood next to her vehicle.

"Tatym!"

Her eyes widened as she scrambled into her truck.

"No." She'd be rammed.

A split second before contact, she sped backward, escaping the collision. A tree took the brunt instead.

Dane and Grayson continued pulling until the entire flatbed sat on the road.

"A close call," Grayson said through his open window. "See you at the house. Unhook us, boys."

Minutes later, Dane pulled onto Tatym's property as she turned around and headed down the mountain. Grayson and his men followed, leaving Dane to complete whatever work he could before taking his grandmother to a doctor's appointment. Only having an hour, all he could do was organize the material and clean up his tools. He hoped the rest of Tatym's day fared better. His would be an unproductive one.

"You look like your milk went past its expiration date," his grandmother said when he entered the house.

He filled her in on the day's happenings. "Want to go to an early supper before your appointment?"

"What part about I rarely leave the house do you not understand?" She frowned.

"You have to leave anyway. Let me change into some clean clothes." He rushed up the stairs and put on clean jeans and a button-up blue plaid shirt.

His grandmother waited by the door, purse in hand. "I still don't like being around a lot of people."

"As if the doctor's office won't be crowded." He planted a kiss on her cheek and opened the door.

She still frowned as she reluctantly entered the diner. A smile soon graced her face as several people called out greetings.

Dane laughed and followed the hostess to a booth. "See? People aren't so bad."

"That is not true." She wiggled her finger at him. "Remember what happened at the ranch just days ago? Or last fall?" She shook her head. "People carry an unbelievable evil."

"Not everyone. Are you evil?"

"I'm sure I carry a seed."

His laughter rang out, attracting Tatym's attention, and she came over. "Grandma, meet Tatym Billings. Tatym, June Mayfield."

"Pleased to meet you, ma'am. Can I bring you something to drink while you look over the menu?"

"I'd like the day's soup and a side salad. You may call me June."

"Don't you want to know what the soup is?" Dane asked.

"I read it on the chalkboard when we entered. It's cheesy potato." She folded her hands on the tabletop. "We don't have a lot of time if we're going to make my appointment."

"I'll have a bacon cheeseburger." Dane declined a menu.

"I'll see if I can put a rush on your order." Tatym smiled and hurried to the kitchen.

"What if one of these people are the town's next killer?" Grandma lowered her voice and arched a brow. "This town is cursed, you know."

"It is not. You have a vivid imagination."

"You'll see. Just wait."

"We're a secluded, small town, high in the mountains, and sometimes it attracts the wrong kind of people. Nothing more than that."

"And your Tatym will be in the middle of it all. Any time a pretty new gal comes to town, trouble shows up."

"Coincidence." He leaned against the back of the booth. His grandmother had said these words several times over the last year or so. After the sheriff who used to be FBI came to town to protect a woman and her mother who were in witness protection—the younger one now the sheriff's wife—Grandma rarely left her house. The following incidents only strengthened her resolve. He was surprised she'd let him take her to supper.

"Hmph." She scrunched her nose. "I have a sense about these things. Someone will come for that rumored deed, and your friend will be in the way."

Someone gasped.

Dane's eyes darted from his grandmother to Tatym who brought their meals. She'd most likely heard most of his conversation with his grandmother. "Never mind her."

"It kind of sounded like a threat." She set Grandma's soup and salad on the table. "Was it?" Her tone had sharpened.

"Of course not, dear." Grandma unwrapped her silverware. "It's a warning."

Chapter Four

Sleep had been a long time coming for Tatym, and she didn't wake in time to watch the mist. The warning from Dane's grandmother, June, had circled her brain like an unbroken movie reel until she'd wanted to bury her face in the pillow and scream.

It was nothing more than an old woman's imagination, but was it? Tatym had no reason to believe the woman's words to be true, yet they nagged at her. Dane had sat there speechless, his eyes wide with shock. That made her feel a little better. He didn't seem to agree with June's viewpoint.

She stretched and contemplated what she'd do on her day off. The garden. There were a few things she could still plant this late in the summer. She tossed off her blanket and prepared for the day, refusing to dwell any more on June's words.

Her resolve went straight out the window when she stepped outside and caught sight of the rabbit hanging from the porch railing. Her blood ran cold. Her heart dropped. This was no death by another animal; this was clearly a warning. June's words rang true.

Dane's truck rumbled up the road and parked near the roofing supplies.

Tatym's legs trembled too much for her to go meet him. Instead, she sagged against the wall of the house.

"What's—" He stopped at the bottom step, his gaze following hers. "I'm calling the sheriff."

"Your grandmother was right." She bent over and tried to regulate her breathing.

"Don't jump to conclusions." He made the call.

"Seriously?" She straightened, her eyes narrowed. "If this isn't a threat, then what would you call it? That's why I find holes dug in my yard. Someone is looking for the deed and wants me out of the way." What would they do if she refused to go? This was her home now. "Please remove the rabbit. I'll make another pot of coffee." Tatym needed something to do.

"I'll remove it after the sheriff arrives."

She nodded and went back into the house. At the sink, she set the coffeepot under running water and planted her hands flat on the edge of the sink. Tatym shuddered as if a cold breeze blew through the house. She didn't realize the pot overflowed until Dane reached around her and shut off the faucet.

"Come here." He turned her and wrapped her in a hug, cradling her head to his chest. After a minute, he led her to a chair. "I'll make the coffee."

She watched as he moved around the kitchen with ease. His strong back muscles rippled under the tee shirt he wore. The tender way he'd held her warmed her heart, dispelling some of the horror of the dead animal outside.

"I thought the deed was just a rumor."

Dane shrugged. "If that is what this is about, then someone believes the rumor to be true."

"What else could it be about? I've only been in town a week. I know a handful of people."

"I don't know, but I don't want you up here alone." He handed her a cup of coffee.

"There's no one to stay with me."

"My grandmother has an extra room."

"No. This is my house, my land." She wouldn't let anyone run her off what was hers.

The sound of an approaching car drew them both outside. The sheriff climbed out of his car and stared at the hanging rabbit. "This is new for this town."

"Yesterday morning, I found a dead possum on my porch. I thought it had been attacked by another animal and crawled up there to die. Now, I'm not so sure." Tatym sat in one of the rockers on the porch. "Plus, I keep finding holes dug in my yard."

"Armadillo?"

"Too big. These holes were made by a shovel." Which meant a person made them. The hand holding the cup trembled. She set the cup on a small table.

"Mind if I take a look around?"

"No." She pushed to her feet to follow.

"You don't have to," Dane said. "I can show him around."

"I know where the holes were dug." Besides, sitting inactive would drive her crazy. "Can we take the rabbit down?"

"Yes." Sheriff Westbrook motioned for her to lead the way.

She showed him where she had filled the holes in. "Dane installed motion lights, but I haven't seen or heard anyone on my property at night."

"I suggest you put up some cameras." He studied the ground where they stood. "Then you'll know exactly what goes on when you're sleeping or working. I'm not seeing anything here to give me a clue."

"Sheriff." Dane's voice came from the front of the house.

Tatym and the sheriff rushed to join him.

Dane peered under the porch on his hands and knees. "Looks like someone has been under here."

"Human?" Sheriff Westbrook hunkered next to him.

Tatym peered between them. Several holes had been dug in the dirt under the porch. Indents showed where someone had knelt. There was no question in her mind someone was searching for something on her property. Something that most likely didn't exist. That made the prospective danger more ominous.

"I'll buy some cameras today."

"Good idea." Dane climbed to his feet. "I'll go with you, but I still think you should move into town until this is resolved."

"I agree," the sheriff said.

"There's been no harm to me." Tatym crossed her arms. "Only to poor animals. Whoever is behind this is trying to run me off not kill me."

~

They were getting smarter by calling the sheriff. He watched them from the trees as they peeked under the porch. The rabbit he'd left lay in the grass waiting to be buried.

He wished he could hear them talking, hear what plans they were making. The temptation to burn down the cabin tugged at him, but what if his grandfather was wrong and the deed was in the cabin? Somehow, he'd have to find a way inside to look around. One day when Tatym was at work he'd break in.

Eventually, he'd have to confront her. Make her too

frightened to stay. Today was not that day.

He turned and walked the half mile to where he'd left his truck, his mind spinning with possible scenarios of how to send that woman named Tatym back to where she belonged and find a way to claim his family's long-lost land.

~

After the sheriff left and Dane buried the rabbit, Dane escorted Tatym to his truck. They'd have to go to Langley in order to purchase the security cameras. "You okay?" He shot her a look over the top of the truck.

"I'm settling down." She climbed inside. "I'll be more prepared if it happens a third time."

He glanced at the roofing materials. Another day of no work on the cabin. If the work didn't get done, he didn't get paid. A heavy rain would cause the aged roof to leak which would cause problems inside the house. Dane exhaled heavily and climbed into the driver's seat.

"What's wrong?" Tatym clicked her seatbelt into place.

"I'm sorry about not starting on the roof."

"That's okay. You don't have to go with me to purchase the cameras. I can drive myself."

"No, I want to make sure you buy the ones you need." He smiled. "I'll work on the roof tomorrow, I promise."

"It's not like you aren't working. You installed the lights, and I'll need you to install the cameras. You can add that to the total I owe you."

Dane turned the truck around and headed down the mountain. He wanted to tell her to keep her money, but starting up a business required funds, something he was short on at the moment. His grandmother had offered to give him the money, saying he'd inherit it when she died anyway, but a man had principles. No handout for him.

"I want to apologize about what my grandmother said at the diner."

"Turns out she was right."

He chuckled. "Don't tell her that. But, seriously, she was out of line saying those things. Ever since the crime started in town, she's become a bit agoraphobic. I can hardly persuade her to leave her house to go to doctor appointments. Convincing her to come to the diner was a miracle. She's forgotten her manners."

Tatym grinned, the color returning to her face. "She's old enough to be allowed to say anything she wants. It did bother me, but after realizing…" she shrugged. "Anyway, it's fine. Eventually whoever is doing the searching will realize nothing is there and give up."

He didn't think so. If someone was crazy enough to believe a rumor that had been circulating for years, they might be capable of just about anything.

At the store, he located cameras that Tatym could check from her laptop or phone. "How many do you think?"

She thought for a minute. "Back of the house, front of the house, maybe one facing the road leading to the cabin? Do you think I should put one under the porch?"

"No, but maybe one inside the house." He grabbed five of the cameras. Better to have an extra than to be short. "Do you need to stop anywhere else?"

"I could do with some groceries for the days I don't work."

"Do you have internet at the cabin? The cameras won't work without it."

"Yes. Grandma liked her social media. It's how we stayed connected." She paid for the purchase, and they drove to the grocery store where she put what he called rabbit food into a cart. "I eat so much heavy food at the diner, I need to eat this on my day off or I'll grow as big as the valley."

"I'll take my chances with the heavy food." Dane gave an exaggerated shudder, glad to see the fear of the morning had left her eyes. He loaded her purchases into the bed of his truck, then drove back to Misty Hollow. As he drove through town, he studied those strolling down the sidewalk. Which one of them had terrorized Tatym? Could it be one of the regulars at the diner? He'd be keeping his eyes and ears peeled. Whoever it was would mess up sooner or later.

He rounded the sharpest curve headed up the mountain. Something darted across the road, then stopped and cowered.

Dane slammed on the brakes, waking the dozing Tatym. The truck skid a short way, then came to a stop. He shoved open his door and raced to the front.

A mixed-breed dog stared up at him with big eyes. It's tail thumped the road despite the fact he could count the dog's ribs.

"Oh, you poor thing." Before Dane could tell her not to, Tatym wrapped her arms around the dog's neck. "Look, Dane. She's starving."

"Covered with fleas and ticks, too, most likely."

"I don't care. She's coming home with us. Let's drop off the groceries and head back down to the pet store."

"Are you sure?" He loved dogs, but strays could be aggressive.

"You said you didn't want me staying alone. What's a better security system than a dog?"

True. "Okay, put her in back. On second thought, put her up front with us, or you won't have any groceries left except for the salad fixings."

Over an hour later, he helped Tatym wash the dog with a shampoo that promised to get rid of ticks and fleas. The dog did not like water, and soon all three of them were dripping.

"Maybe we should've fed her first." Tatym wiped her face with a towel. "I didn't want her in the house until she was clean."

"What are you going to name her?"

"Now that I see how glossy black her hair is, I think Ebony is the perfect name."

As if she knew what her new role in life was, Ebony stared toward the woods behind the house and growled.

Chapter Five

Dane stepped in front of Tatym. "Go in the house."

She gripped the dog's collar and shoved at the stubborn man in front of her. "I'm going to let her go. We'll follow." Who was he to tell her to go in the house?

He whipped around. "Are you serious?"

"Absolutely." She gave a nod and released the dog. "Get 'em." She had no idea whether the dog knew what the command meant, but she took off like a cheetah.

"Come on." Dane grabbed her hand and pulled her after him.

"We can run better if you let go of me." Tatym's short legs were no match for his longer ones.

"What if we get separated?"

"I know my way home." She yanked free and bent at the waist to catch her breath. "Don't wait on me."

Ebony's barks rang through the trees.

"Nope. Not going anywhere without you."

Fine. Tatym straightened and darted in the direction of the barks.

A man shouted in the distance. A shot rang out.

"Ebony." Her name slipped from Tatym's lips like a hoarse whisper. Had she gotten a dog only to have her taken away? Fear spurred her to run faster.

Dane jerked her back. "If the person we're chasing has a gun, which it appears they do, we can't barge in on them. I don't feel like dying today." He turned her to face him. "Got it?"

"Got it." She frowned. "But I need to make sure my dog is okay."

"She is. Listen."

Tatym stood still. Ebony had resumed her barking. They had to grab the dog before the next shot took her life.

Dane took her hand again and led her at a slower pace deeper into the woods.

Where did the man come from? Why wouldn't he leave her alone? Tatym owned the cabin and the land fair and square. It had been in her family's possession for a hundred years at least. Her lungs burned, her legs on fire. "I can't." She was no match for Dane's long-legged sprint.

She stumbled only to be hauled back up by Dane who, thankfully, slowed his pace. "Whistle for…her."

"Great idea." He stopped and put two fingers in his mouth, letting loose an ear-piercing whistle. "Hopefully, she knows it means to come."

Ebony did. Less than a minute later, Tatym's muscles clenched as something crashed through the brush toward them. She relaxed when Ebony came into sight. "What a good girl you are. Let's go home and feed you." She ruffled the dog's fur, then glanced at Dane. "What now?"

"It's starting to get dark, so we can't continue. We'll call the sheriff, again, and let him take over."

"Might as well put him on speed dial."

He grinned. "I do. I'll tell you all about the trouble on the ranch when there's time."

She'd forgotten he used to be a cowboy.

A car engine rumbled past the trees. They'd been so close to whoever insisted on terrorizing Tatym. If the cameras had been working, they'd have the guy on film. She asked if Dane could installed them while she fixed them something to eat.

"I will. It's getting dark, but I have a headlamp. I'll rest easier knowing you have the lights, camera, and the dog."

She would too. Tatym hadn't bought just salad fixings; she bought a couple of steaks, some canned goods, and potatoes. They'd have steak and a small salad. That way, they'd all be happy.

When they arrived at the cabin, Tatym led Ebony inside while Dane got to work. The man worked too much, but it was always because she needed something. She'd never met such a bossy yet unself-absorbed man in her life. Nor had she ever immediately felt as safe as she did with him. What she felt for Dane had nothing to do with his physical appearance. It didn't matter that he dwarfed her. What did matter was that he wouldn't hesitate to keep her from harm.

Because of her petite size, men seemed to want to lord it over her or call her stupid names like spider monkey or some such idiocy. Dane was different. He'd try to boss her around but didn't push the issue when she shoved back. Why hadn't she met anyone like him before?

She glanced out the window as a ladder slammed against the wall. Then, a jean-clad Dane— jeans that fit in all the right places—climbed the ladder. He smiled as he passed the window, then continued until the only thing Tatym could see was his chiseled chest. He'd removed his shirt. Tatym swallowed against a suddenly dry throat, let her gaze roam over the view, then stepped reluctantly away from the window. She didn't like to be ogled, so she wouldn't do it to someone else no matter how good they looked.

When the steaks were done, she knocked on the window to catch his attention. "Food's ready."

He leaned down, nodded, then climbed from the ladder, donning his shirt as he entered the house, leaving the front door open. A nice breeze drifted through the house. Thank goodness for that shirt. She wasn't sure she'd be able to eat if she sat across from a bare-chested Dane. One would think she'd never seen a handsome man's chest before. Well, she hadn't seen one quite as fine as his.

Her gaze roamed over hair the color of wheat, eyes as blue as the summer sky. A cleft in his chin and a jaw that wore a bit of late-afternoon stubble. Oh, yes, this man was fine.

"What's wrong?" He tilted his head. "You look as if you're miles away."

Her face heated as she set a plate on the table in front of him. "Just thinking about the day."

"It's on my mind, too. I'm thinking we need to set a trap."

"What kind?" She took her own plate and sat.

"I'm going to—"

"Do what, Dane?" Sheriff Westbrook stood in the doorway. "Please do tell us what plan you've concocted."

~

Busted. Dane gave a grin. "How 'bout I let on that while doing renovations around here, I stumbled across something of interest? I won't go into too much detail. Just enough to tickle folks' imaginations."

"That will put the target on you." Tatym shook her head. "Can I get you something to eat, Sheriff?"

"No, thanks. I've already eaten, but that coffee smells good."

She got up and poured him a cup before returning to her meal. "Then, we'll both be in danger. I don't like that idea."

"Tell me why I'm here again?" the sheriff quipped. "I've news of my own you'll be interested in. And who is this raven-haired beauty?"

"My new dog, Ebony. We almost ran over her on the way home. She was covered in fleas and ticks. Since she was obviously uncared for, she's now mine." Tatym pursed her lips.

"Fine by me." The sheriff chuckled.

"After we arrived home after purchasing dog supplies, Ebony's hackles raised, and she growled toward the trees. Tatym released her and she took off. We heard a man yell followed by a gunshot, then a car engine roared to life."

"Could've been anyone. The road past that bit of forest is a common one." The sheriff took a sip of his coffee. "They could've gone exploring and stumbled across your place."

"We'd believe that if not for the dead animals." Dane stabbed a piece of steak. "No one has died. I'd like to keep it that way."

"That might not be entirely true." Sheriff Westbrook released his breath in a long sigh. "Was your grandmother a diabetic, Tatym?"

"Not that I know of. Why?"

"It appears your grandmother died of severe hypoglycemia or insulin shock. Both of which can cause death by overdose. If your grandmother wasn't diabetic, then—"

"Why too much insulin?" Tatym's hand paused halfway to her mouth. Lettuce and a slice of cucumber fell back to her plate. "You think she was murdered?"

He shrugged. "I might not have thought too much about it if you weren't being hassled. Leading this person to think you might have the deed isn't a good idea. If I'm right about Ms. Billings being killed, then the unsub won't hesitate to kill again."

Tatym's fork clattered on her plate. "I never suspected foul play. They told me she died of a heart attack."

"Also caused by too much insulin." The sheriff rose to his feet. "Are the cameras installed?"

"Almost. I'll finish putting up the last one before I go home," Dane said, standing.

"I need to recommend, Tatym, that you not stay up here or at least not alone. Good night." He turned and strode from the cabin.

"Are you okay?" Dane glanced at Tatym. The sheriff had laid quite the bombshell on her. "Yes."

She raised red-rimmed eyes. "Could someone really have killed my grandmother? Does the perp think the deed is reason enough to kill?"

"Maybe." He pulled her into a hug, rubbing her trembling back with his hand. "Do you want me to stay here tonight?"

"No. I have Ebony and the cameras."

Turned down because of a dog. He smiled and stepped back. "I can be here in twenty minutes if you need me. After I put up that last camera, I'll show you how to use them, then head home. Tomorrow, I'll be here before you leave for work."

"I'd hope so. I don't go in until ten." She gave a shaky smile and started clearing the table.

Outside, Dane stopped and stared in the direction of the woods, thankful the back camera was already installed. He didn't relish a bullet in the back. Dane grabbed the ladder and carried it to the front of the cabin. Unless they climbed up from the valley, no one would be able to surprise him. Flicking on his headlamp, he went to work more determined than ever to find out who bothered Tatym. He'd do whatever it took to keep her safe. Even sleep in his truck nearby at night.

~

She had a dog? He shouldn't have missed, but the thing was right on his heels. He'd barely escaped. If someone hadn't whistled, he'd bear the mark of the dog's teeth on his leg.

How could he get close to the cabin now? The dog would sound the alarm at the sight or smell of him. He wouldn't be able to resume digging for the deed. If Tatym was out of the picture, he'd bulldoze the place to find what he needed. Without that deed in hand, getting possession of the land would be impossible. There'd be no high-class resort to make him wealthy.

Not to mention Dane hanging around all the time. Well, Tatym was wasting her money on renovations. The house wouldn't be standing much longer.

He climbed out of his truck and slammed the door as he headed for his house. "Becky, I'm home."

"I've kept your supper warm. The boys are already in bed." She studied his face long enough to make him squirm. "You look as if you've had a rough day."

"Very. Was chased by a dog."

She gave him a tender kiss on his cheek. "I don't understand why people can't chain up their dogs when you're doing work for them. Have a seat. I'll bring your supper and a drink."

His sweet wife and his boys were why he persisted. They deserved the life he should be able to give them. For far too long, others had reaped the benefits of what his family had started so long ago.

He stared at his wife's slender back. No matter what he had to do, he'd do it for her. The hard thing was not letting her find out. If she did, she'd leave him and take his sons. And he couldn't allow that to happen.

Chapter Six

Tatym opened her front door and peeked out. No dead animal awaited her on the porch. She stepped out and surveyed the dark lawn, then headed for the overlook, stopping halfway. In her not-fully-awake-yet state, she hadn't noticed Dane's truck sitting where he'd parked it the day before.

"Come on, Ebony." One hand clutching her cup of coffee, she moved slowly toward the truck fearing the worst. Had the person haunting her harmed Dane?

Her heart lodged in her throat only to be replaced by irritation. The fogged-up window wasn't caused by a dead man. She rapped on the window.

The window rolled down. "I thought I'd be up by the time you came out." He gave a sheepish grin.

"You slept out here?" She posted her fists on her hips. "Are you serious?" Forget everything she'd said about him not being heavy-handed. She turned and marched to the overlook.

A few seconds later, Dane joined her. "You're up early."

"I try to be out here every morning to watch the sun rise." She lifted her cup to her lips. "There's coffee in the house."

"Don't be mad—"

"Shh." She didn't want anything to mar the beauty of the sun on the mist. No talking, just peace. It was too late for her not to be upset—and the presence of his truck had already done that. Her eyes closed, she took a fortifying breath, opening them again as the mist dissipated. The beauty began to lift some of her irritation at seeing Dane sleeping in his truck. Once the mist was gone, she whipped around and headed back to the house, Ebony and Dane following.

"Look, I'm sorry," Dane said, closing the door behind them. "I didn't want you here alone."

"I have Ebony." She fought to keep the harshness from her words. "Don't take away my independence. I've been alone for a long time now and managed to take care of myself."

"Did you have someone—a potentially violent someone—try to run you off your property before?" He crossed his arms. "Don't forget that the sheriff suspects your aunt was murdered."

As if she could. "There was no animal left on my porch this morning. Maybe he gave up."

"You don't really believe that."

"No." She poured him a cup of coffee, then took a seat at the table. "Still, you shouldn't have stayed."

"I thought I'd be up working before you came out." He sat across from her.

"That does not make it any better. You only planned on being sneakier."

He shrugged. "I already explained myself. Any plans before work?"

"I'm going to put in my summer garden." She'd have a couple of hours before needing to shower and leave. Hopefully, digging in the soil would take away the last vestiges of her irritation.

"I'll start on the roof. If we don't have any more setbacks, I should finish by the end of the day tomorrow. We can meet together then and see what needs doing in here."

"The kitchen. Everything needs to be replaced. I'll collect some photos of what I want." She finished her coffee and headed outside. Tatym hated feeling ill toward Dane. It had put off her entire morning.

She gathered the tools she'd need from the garage and headed to the patch of ground she planned to turn into a garden. Ebony watched as she jabbed the shovel into the ground. "Don't get any ideas, Eb. I don't want any unplanned digging in my garden." That included whoever dug holes around her property.

She glanced to where Dane worked on the roof, having torn up more than half of it, then up at the darkening sky. The rain would halt progress. Again. All she could do was hope the roof didn't leak too bad.

After digging up weeds and hoeing her rows, Tatym headed to the shower. She'd plant the saplings she planned on picking up during her break before the supper rush. After a shower, she grabbed a banana and an apple from the bowl in the middle of the table and rushed outside. "Please don't fall off the roof," she called out as she raced to her truck. Her time in the garden had made her run late.

"Going to rain soon. I'll be putting down a tarp. See you later."

As she reached the halfway mark down the mountain, the skies opened and delivered a deluge. Tatym could barely see through the heavy rain. She slowed her speed and tried to see with the aid of the windshield wipers. Now she'd be late for sure.

A shriek escaped her as her back tires slid into the ditch. Tatym pressed the gas pedal. The wheels spun and sank. Great. She turned on her blinkers, then grabbed her phone and called work.

Headlights. She straightened as the truck slowed and rolled down her window. Water ran down the inside of the door.

Mr. Grayson, owner of the construction business, rolled down his window. "Hold tight. I'll pull you out. Good thing I was headed your way to drop off some bolts we left out of the delivery."

"Thanks." She rolled up her window and dried the door with her apron.

After Grayson turned around up the road, he came back and stopped in front of Tatym's truck. He hooked a heavy chain to her car and gave her a thumbs-up.

What did that mean? That he was going to pull now? Or did it mean he wanted her to wait a minute? The sudden jerk as Grayson moved forward answered her question. Once free of the ditch, she waited while her truck was unhooked. Then, with a honk of her horn, she continued on to work.

~

Dane stepped onto the front porch as Grayson drove up in front of him. "Hey."

Grayson nodded. "Didn't expect to see you here on a day like this."

"The rain isn't supposed to last more than an hour or two." He tilted his head. "Is there something I can help you with?"

"Bolts we forgot to give you." He tossed a bag to

Dane.

He caught it, surprised by the weight. "You did give me everything I need. I double-checked." Dane stepped forward to return the bolts.

"Somebody messed up then." Grayson gave a thin-lipped smile. "Good to know." He drove around the house and out of sight.

Since Dane had at least an hour before the rain stopped, he figured it was a good time to put his plan into place. First stop, his grandmother. For a woman who rarely left the house, she seemed to know everything there was to know about everyone in town.

"What do you mean you believe the stories?" Grandma frowned at him over the rim of her teacup.

"I've seen evidence." Dane grinned. He'd make up for the lies later.

Her face scrunched. "Fine. You have a reason for this nonsense." She set her cup on the saucer. "I'll spread the news around."

"How do you do that?" How did she always know when he lied?

"You're just like me. All I have to do is trade places. Then, it's as plain as day."

He laughed. "Yes, please spread the word through whatever grapevine you use." The rain had slowed to a drizzle. Dane drove slowly past the diner and waved at Tatym who glanced out the window. He parked in front of the hardware store.

A bell jingled as he opened the store door. "Hey, Herb." He smiled at the man behind the counter. "Just here to pick up a couple of things. I have a lot of digging to do."

"What are you digging up?"

"Treasure." Dane grabbed a shovel and a pickax.

"You're working on Alice's house, aren't you? The place where there's some other deed to the property?" He shook his head. "I thought you were smarter than that, Dane."

"It'll be fun." He paid for his purchases and headed back to the cabin. Between Grandma and Herb, everyone would soon know Dane thought the deed existed and had evidence to prove the fact. The race to find the deed would begin in earnest. The bad guy would make a mistake and be arrested for trespassing and, if what the sheriff believed was true, murder.

With the rain stopped, Dane finished preparing the roof for the metal the next day. Tatym wouldn't be home for another two hours. Should he stay and share diner leftovers again, or go home and give her some space after the morning they'd had?

He didn't want to smother her, only keep her safe. Dane hadn't had a lot of experience with women. Ranching didn't allow much free time. Now with his own business, he could play around with the idea of a relationship. Problem was—he had a perfect possibility to fill that role right in front of him, and he'd already done something stupid to mess it all up.

Go home, it was. He made sure the tarp was secure on the roof, gathered up his tools, and checked to ensure Ebony was safely in the house. Then, he headed home to *Wheel of Fortune* and Grandma.

"Didn't think you'd be home again." She glanced over her shoulder from her seat in front of the TV. "It's shameful, if you ask me."

"I slept in my truck."

She cackled. "Now that I think on it, of course you

did."

His frow furrowed. What was she talking about? "You're stranger every day. Some of the things you say—"

"At my age, I can say whatever is on my mind. Now, hush. I'm watching my show."

"Have you eaten?"

"Not yet." She waved for him to go away.

Laughing, he went to the kitchen and opened the fridge. Plenty of eggs. He'd make them each an omelet. When he finished, he carried the plates into the living room just as a crime show came on. They didn't eat in the dining room on Wednesday. That's when his grandmother's favorite shows were on.

During a commercial, she turned her attention his way. "I heard Alice may have been killed."

"How'd you hear that?"

"From someone who heard it from the receptionist at the sheriff's office. Which means it's most likely true."

"Pure speculation at this point. Tell your friends not to interfere in the sheriff's investigation."

"Why would they do that?"

His eyes narrowed. "Because y'all are friends and will want to help the sheriff solve the death of another friend." He wagged his finger between him and her. "Two peas in a pod, remember?"

He cleaned up the dishes and went upstairs to his room and sat at the desk. It was time to go over his measurements again. Unfortunately, he couldn't order anything because he'd left without speaking to Tatym and had no idea what style of appliances she wanted.

Sometime later, Dane heard his grandmother shuffle

off to bed. He'd better turn in so he could arrive up the mountain at a reasonable time. Dane almost hoped for more distractions so he had a reason to see Tatym for a while. Once the job was finished, would she go on a date with him if he asked?

He stripped down and climbed into bed, folding his arms behind his head. One to two days to do the roof…it would take a week to do the kitchen, provided the appliances arrived on time. One more week to have a reason to see her. One more week to keep a protective eye on her. Dane rolled over to his side and stared at the cell phone lying on the nightstand. What would she say if he called her to say good night? To hear her voice and know she was safe.

At that moment, his phone rang, the screen showing Tatym's number—as if she'd heard him. "Good evening." He smiled and rolled back.

"Someone is in my yard," she whispered. "They don't seem to care about the lights."

Chapter Seven

"Make sure the doors are locked." Dane scrambled to get dressed. "Hide in the bathroom. Barricade the door." He'd never reach her in time. Dressed, he slipped his bare feet into slippers, grabbed his keys off the nightstand, his gun from the drawer, and clamored from the house. *I'm coming, Tatym.* As he drove, he placed a 9-1-1 call in hopes the authorities would either beat him there or arrive around the same time.

The half-hour drive seemed like an hour. Rather than drive to the cabin, he stopped a football field's length away and quietly slid out of his truck and closed the door.

Clutching his gun, he slipped into the trees to come up behind the house and hopefully get to the intruder before he was spotted. The previous day's rain had softened the ground underfoot making quiet movement possible.

Ebony's barks ricocheted from the house. The sound seemed to come from the bathroom. The intruder would know exactly where Tatym hid.

Dane stopped and studied the expanse of lawn illuminated by the moon. The light on the front of the house flicked on. A dark figure of a man turned the corner, and the back light came on. He circled the house. Why?

The arrival of a squad car sent the figure darting into the woods. Dane rushed toward the house.

"Stop right there or I will shoot." Two deputies hunkered behind car doors, their weapons aimed at Dane.

"Not me. The guy ran into the woods." He wished Sheriff Westbrook would have been the one to respond to his call. He didn't know these two.

"Drop your weapon and put your hands behind your head."

Dane complied. "You have the wrong guy. The one you want is getting away."

"On your knees."

He sighed and dropped to his knees. "I'm the one who called you guys. Call the sheriff. He'll vouch for me."

"Dane?" Tatym and Ebony stood on the front porch. "What's going on? Where's the other guy?"

"He ran off." Dane glared at the deputies.

"This isn't the intruder." Tatym moved toward him.

"Stop right there, ma'am. We need to verify your ID." One of them lowered his weapon and stepped in front of her.

"It's in the house." She turned and led him inside, leaving Dane kneeling in the damp grass. They returned a few minutes later, and the officer ordered Dane to show his identification. "I left it at home. I do have my registration in the glove compartment."

"You left it at home?" The deputy stared down at him.

"I was too busy worrying about my friend. Call the

sheriff. He'll vouch for me. Can I get up now?"

"Yes, but stay here." The deputy returned to the car and placed a call on the radio.

Dane stared in the direction the man had gone—he was bound to be miles away by now. He turned back to Tatym. "Are you all right?"

"I'm fine. Thank you for coming." She stepped into his arms and wrapped hers around his waist.

"We'd like to ask you some questions, ma'am."

Dane reluctantly released her, then turned to Ebony. "Stay, girl." The dog whined but stayed by his side while Tatym followed the officers. He picked up his weapon. While the deputies were occupied, he had something to do. "Come on." Turning in the direction the hooded man had gone, he jogged with Ebony padding by his side.

One of the deputies yelled for him to stop, then caught up with him. "If what you say is true, you shouldn't be heading out there by yourself. Or with me for that matter."

Dane glanced at the man's name on his shirt. "I appreciate it, Deputy Johnson."

"Stay behind me." The deputy moved in front of him, his flashlight aimed at the ground. "Are you sure there was an intruder?"

"You can look at the camera footage when we return." Of course, he was sure. He'd seen the man with his own eyes.

Tracks stopped in the same place as last time. "We've followed someone's tracks to this spot before." Dane glanced up and down the fire road. "Can the department send someone out here for when he returns?"

"What makes you think he'll return?"

"Because he has every night since Tatym took

ownership." He shook his head and returned to the house. "The deputies should see the camera footage," he said to Tatym.

She nodded and pushed up from her seat on the sofa. "I'll get my laptop."

A few minutes later, the four of them stared at the screen as a man in a ski mask and dark hoodie circled the house. "Why didn't he try to break in?" Tatym glanced from Dane to the deputies. "Why go in circles."

"Intimidation." Eventually, he'd realize Tatym wouldn't be frightened away. That would be when the man would move to the next step. "No arguments. I'm moving into your guest room until this man is caught."

She opened her mouth to say something, then snapped it closed.

~

He laughed with glee on his way to the Langley hotel he favored when he needed Becky to believe he was out of town. If only he could have seen the look on Tatym's face as she cowered in the bathroom listening to her dog's barks echo off the tiles. The sound had been loud outside, so he could only imagine how they'd made her ears ring.

When he arrived at the hotel, he sent his wife a text saying he'd had a long day…not a lie…and he'd see her for supper the next day. He quickly added an "I love you and kiss the kids" before undressing and heading for the shower. The ski mask and hoodie weren't exactly summer attire.

As he showered, his mind spun with more ideas to terrorize the latest squatter on his family's land. He'd have to up his game and make her more frightened, until she left. Surely, she couldn't be as tough as her grandmother. If so, she'd meet the same fate.

He'd seen her standing on the overlook most mornings. It wouldn't be hard to stage an accident. No way she'd survive the fall.

Exhaustion erased the thrill of the evening. He'd been out late too many nights in a row. His sore back made him realize he wasn't as young as he used to be. He missed his wife and sons.

He crawled into bed without bothering to get dressed. Maybe he'd take a few days off and let Tatym and her cowboy bodyguard think he'd stopped. The sheriff's department didn't cause a moment's worry. Sheriff Westbrook was stretched thin, and his two rookie deputies were as bad as Laurel and Hardy. Didn't know their head from a tree limb.

He folded his arms behind his head. Yep, he had no worries. Dane didn't have the real deed. Or did he? He frowned. If he had found it, he could destroy the very evidence that would prove who the rightful owner was. That could not happen. He needed to find out.

~

Another long, restless night caused Tatym to oversleep. She woke to the delicious aroma of brewing coffee and frying bacon. Bacon? She hadn't bought bacon.

She thrust open her door to the sight of a shirtless Dane in baggy shorts standing at the stove. "Where did the bacon come from?"

"All you had was rabbit food, mostly, so I grabbed some food when I packed a bag of clothes." He grinned over his shoulder. "Now, we'll both be happy."

Not until a particular spooky someone stopped coming around. She grabbed a protein drink from the fridge and sat at the table. Again, she'd slept though the mist. "So, how long until he makes a move to hurt me?"

Dane's hand holding the tongs froze in midair. "When he realizes he can't scare you away."

She dropped her gaze to the table. "I won't run."

"I'm sure your grandmother felt the same way." He returned to the sizzling bacon.

"It's someone I've met. I'm sure. Someone who has been to this house, to the diner." All she had to do was keep her eyes open for anyone who showed her a lot of attention.

"I agree. How 'bout I follow you to work, then be there to follow you home?"

"What about your work?"

"I'll finish up the roof today."

She stood and retrieved the photos of appliances and rooms she'd printed out as examples. "I want these. The kitchen can be done with white cabinets and cement countertops. I'd like a small peninsula at the end to give me more counter space. Can you do that?"

He glanced at the photos. "Sure. Shouldn't take more than a week once the appliances arrive. It will look pretty. Very modern. I thought you'd want to keep the rustic-cabin look."

"I want a kitchen that is going to last for a very long time." Tatym resumed her seat. "Modern rustic." She smiled and finished her drink before getting up again. "I've an early shift today, but I'm off at three." No sense telling him not to be there. When he made his mind up, nothing could deter him.

As she drove to work, she glanced repeatedly in her rearview mirror to see Dane following. Ebony's black head hung out the passenger-side window, her gaze locked on Tatym's car. The sweet thing had wanted nothing more than to bust through the wall of the bathroom and grab whoever had been outside. Her thoughts went to the camera footage. The man's build seemed familiar, which led her to believe she'd seen him. Maybe even spoke to him.

Not a thin man or overweight but stocky. Maybe five ten, two hundred pounds. Not muscled, a slight paunch. But that could have been from an oversized hoodie. "I'll find out who you are eventually," she said out loud. "And when I do, I'll make sure you're locked up for a long time." Tatym wasn't sure how exactly, but she'd figure out a way. She refused to live her life in fear waiting for the man to make a move.

Dane had the right idea about starting a new rumor, and she heard all about it when she arrived at work.

"Did Dane James really find the other deed?" Heather followed her into the employee room behind the kitchen.

"He thinks so." Tatym locked up her purse. "At least, I think he knows where it is or suspects."

"What if it proves you aren't the rightful owner?"

"It would have to prove so, without a doubt, which I don't think it will. That land has been in my family for a very long time." She donned her apron and returned to the front, Heather on her heels.

"But what if?"

"Then I'll figure it out then." She pulled her order pad from her pocket and went to greet her first diner. "Good morning, Mr. Grayson. What can I bring you?"

"Chicken fried steak with biscuits, gravy, and eggs. Got a busy day ahead of me. And keep the coffee coming."

"Late night?" She arched a brow and smiled.

He rolled his eyes. "A few late ones. Owning a construction business doesn't always keep nine-to-five hours."

"I wouldn't think so. I'll be right back with your coffee."

As the day went on, she took the opportunity to linger at the table of every man who dined alone to determine if he could be her nighttime stalker. She ruled out the young and the very old, focusing on those who seemed to fit the body type. There were a lot of candidates.

Finding out who wanted to run her off wouldn't be easy. But Tatym took after her grandmother and running away from a problem wasn't in her vocabulary. Besides, she needed to determine whether her grandmother had been murdered.

Because if she didn't, she'd share the same fate.

Chapter Eight

Three days of work, and she still had no idea who could be hanging around her place. Nor had the person shown up again. The customers in the diner were regulars. People she saw every day. One of them couldn't be trying to run her off her land, or could they?

She discounted the elderly men at the counter. Neither Walt nor Wilbur could move fast enough to escape Ebony. She also discounted the women. It had definitely been a man she'd seen on the camera footage.

Dane and his grandmother entered the diner. Tatym flashed them a smile and delivered a plate of eggs and bacon to a customer before waiting on the new arrivals.

"Good morning." Dane had told her his grandmother had another appointment and that he'd be late starting work on her kitchen.

"Coffee?"

"Two. Black, please." June held up two fingers. "Glad to see you haven't been scared away."

Tatym frowned. "It would take more than someone wandering onto my property to get rid of me." She bit her lip, wondering whether she should bring up her grandmother's possible murder.

"Spit it out, dear, before you gnaw a hole in your

bottom lip." June tilted her head, one penciled brow arched.

"This isn't the place," Dane said. "Maybe Tatym could come over after her shift?" He glanced her way.

"Sure." Tatym nodded. "I'll bring a pie." If anyone besides the sheriff suspected foul play in her grandmother's death, it would be June. She studied every face that entered the diner until her shift ended at seven. Then after purchasing an apple pie from the bakery down the street, she headed to June's house.

Dane's truck sat parked in the driveway. Good. She didn't think she could handle June's forthright manner alone. The woman spoke her mind more than anyone Tatym had ever met.

Squaring her shoulders, she pressed the doorbell.

Dane, a dishtowel slung over his shoulder, opened the door. "Thank goodness. Grandma has been pestering me all day about what you want to talk about."

So, it wasn't just Tatym she unnerved. "Here to the rescue. Apple."

"I'm glad you didn't get pecan." June dried wet hands on an old-fashioned, cotton apron. "This might be the South, but pecan pie is too sweet for my taste."

Tatym shot Dane a smile and followed the other woman to a dinette set in the kitchen that looked straight out of a 1950s catalogue. She set the pie in the center of the table and sat.

June had three plates and utensils ready. "Cut us each a slice, Dane, and don't be skimpy. I ate a salad for supper for a reason."

He laughed and served the pie. "Busy day at the diner?"

"The restaurant is always busy." Tatym wanted to

slump in her seat to take some pressure off her aching back but somehow didn't believe June would approve of slouching. Why did it bother her so much what the woman thought of her? She glanced at Dane. Because she liked him so much? Maybe.

"Are you going to tell me what's on your mind or not, dear?" June forked a bite of pie into her mouth.

"Do you find anything suspicious about my grandmother's death?"

"Dane did mention the other evening the sheriff department thought it might not be a heart attack." She set down her fork. "I didn't question her death at the time, although it saddened me that my strong friend would succumb so quickly to a heart attack when she'd shown no signs before of heart trouble."

"Do you think murder was possible?"

"Of course. Look at how hard someone is working to run you off. Alice would not have run either. That's why I'm going to have Dane stay at your place until this is over."

Dane's eyes widened. "When were you going to tell me this?"

"Don't act so surprised. You slept in your truck one night. Might as well move to the guestroom. This creep might stop if there's a man on the premises."

Hmph. A woman such as herself could handle a nuisance, especially since she had a big dog, but she had called Dane when she'd spotted the man. She sighed and returned to eating her pie. "I'll leave that decision up to Dane."

"I'll try not to be any trouble." He frowned. "Staying there will allow me to finish your kitchen faster."

"Sorry. I don't mean to sound rude or ungrateful. It's just that I don't like feeling helpless. I've been on my own for years and don't like the idea that I need a man to keep me safe." She shoved her plate aside.

"Sometimes, we all need someone's help," he said softly, also pushing aside his empty plate.

~

Dane hadn't expected Grandma's idea of him staying in Tatym's cabin to ruin her evening. He tossed some things into a duffel bag with more force than necessary. Couldn't Tatym see the safety in him being under the same roof? When he'd finished packing, he headed downstairs and joined her in the kitchen where she cleaned the dishes from the pie. "I'm ready to follow you home."

She dried her hands on a towel. "I walked here. My truck is at the diner."

"Then I'll give you a ride there." Obstinate or not, he didn't want her to be alone. Not for a second. She'd have to get used to the idea of having him around.

Her eyes flashed, but she didn't argue. "I understand." Shoulders slumped, she said goodbye to his grandmother and headed for the door.

Grandma put a hand on his arm. "She's an independent woman who now has a babysitter. Be patient with her. It isn't that she doesn't like you. Quite the contrary, if you ask me."

"Good night." He placed a kiss on her cheek. "Call me if you need to. You'll always be my best girl."

"Not for long, I wager. Go on now. She's outside alone."

Exactly what he didn't want. "I'll see you tomorrow." He rushed to join Tatym on the porch. After a quick glance around, he marched to the truck and opened the door for her, tossing his bag inside.

The short ride to where she'd left her vehicle was made in silence. He wanted to ask her what she was thinking, but the serious expression on her face kept his mouth shut. All the way up the mountain, his mind whirled to come up with the words to soothe her ruffled emotions. How would she react when he followed her to work in the morning, then home from work?

With a resigned glance his way, Tatym opened the truck door the instant he cut the engine. "I'll put clean sheets on the guest bed."

"I can do that. The linen closet, right?" He followed her up the front porch, studying the area as he did. He'd bring Ebony out to look around, then pull up the camera footage. His steps faltered. This was not his house. He wasn't law enforcement. It was not his place to make any plans without consulting Tatym.

"Are you coming?" She glanced over her shoulder as she unlocked the door.

"Do you mind if I take Ebony around the perimeter, then check the camera footage?"

"Sure, and I can check the footage." She called for Ebony.

Dane set his bag on the porch and motioned for the dog to go with him. He grabbed a flashlight from the cab of his truck and headed for the edge of the tree line. That's where the intruder kept coming from.

Lights flickered on in the house, casting yellow boxes across the lawn.

Ebony stopped, her ears pricking forward, then continued on with her nose to the ground. Dane kept his ears and eyes peeled. The dog would alert him if anyone was around, but he still didn't want to be caught unawares.

A clean sweep of the cleared land and a few feet into the trees revealed nothing. Dane frowned. Why had the man stopped coming around? Could he have a job that required travel? That might help narrow down some suspects. He'd bring up the idea with the sheriff after he followed Tatym to work in the morning.

"Nothing on the cameras," Tatym said when he entered through the back door.

"Nothing outside either." He told her his suspicion.

"Or maybe he was in an accident. There was one on the interstate a few days ago." She leaned her back against the counter, arms crossed. "The danger could be past. If nothing happens within a day or two, I'm sure your grandmother will allow you to go home."

Dane met her body language with the same. "She *let* me come now, but don't you agree there is safety in numbers? Don't forget your grandmother most likely was murdered. Here. In this cabin." He regretted the words at once as her face paled.

"How can I possibly forget that? Her death is what brought me here to be harassed by someone who believes in a stupid rumor."

"I'm sorry." He ran both hands through his hair. "We're both tired. Things will look different in the morning."

"You're going to follow me to work, aren't you?"

"Yes." He speared her gaze with his own. "Until not only us but the sheriff believes the danger is past, I'll be your shadow."

"Okay." She pressed her lips together and nodded. "I appreciate your concern. Good night."

He stared after her. Why the sudden acceptance of his being here? What could she be planning? Dane stepped onto the front porch to retrieve his bag. Gripping the handle, he stared toward the cliff. In the morning he'd join Tatym for the show.

~

Looks like the cowboy planned on sticking around. He lowered the binoculars. It might be time to start making himself known again. Why let Dane James waste his time? He laughed, raising the eyepiece again.

Dane went back into the cabin. A few minutes later, the lights turned off in the front part of the house, and the bedroom lights came on. First hers, then his. Yes, he'd found a way inside. Silly Alice had hidden a key in the body of a ceramic ladybug under her hydrangea bush. He knew where everything was inside that cabin.

He knew she liked to eat healthy, what kind of perfume she wore…which was a big mistake. Knowing Tatym too well would make his quest more difficult. It was better to think of her as an obstacle rather than a person. That would make getting rid of her easier if she didn't choose to sell out.

He lowered the binoculars again and backed down the road, not bothering to turn on his headlights until he rounded a slight curve. Branches scratched the sides of his truck as he turned around on the narrow dirt road, which sent shudders down his back at the screechy sound.

Lingering there and dwelling on the future would make him late getting home. He promised Becky he'd be home before the children went to bed. Someday though, when the resort replaced Tatym's cabin, he'd make it up to his wife. Becky would be a wealthy woman.

What he needed now was a quick, foolproof plan to get rid of a stubborn young woman.

Chapter Nine

Frank Grayson rapped his knuckles on the window of Dane's truck.

Dane rolled down his window. "What's up?"

"There's a rumor going around town that you know where the original deed to the Billings land is." The man grinned.

Since the original resided in a safe-deposit box at the bank, he sure did. "You know how rumors are. Most don't have enough concrete to set a stick."

"You don't seem the type to start a rumor, but word came straight from your grandma's mouth."

Dane gave what he hoped was a sly smile. "I might have an inkling." He reached for the key in the ignition as a couple of other men slowed to listen. "I'm sure everyone will know if I find the location." Since his ploy sparked interest in the residents of Misty Hollow, he'd set a few more subtle clues to lure Tatym's intruder into the open.

A woman stepped next to Grayson, giving Dane his opportunity to escape more questions. Tatym's countertop had arrived, and he needed to pick it up from the warehouse in Langley. This would give him another opportunity to let it slip he knew more than he did.

He stopped at the gas station to top off his tank.

The man at the next pump gave him a head nod. After a few seconds, he said, "Are you Dane James?"

"I am."

"Heard you found a deed."

"Strong possibility." He inserted his card into the machine, paid for his gas, and climbed back into his truck. Word was spreading faster than he'd anticipated.

At the warehouse, he waited for his order to be retrieved from the back. He made a fake phone call within hearing distance of the receptionist. "I'm pretty sure I know where the deed is. It will prove once and for all who the real owner of that property on Misty Mountain is…Yes, I know." He cut the woman a glance and turned his back. "I'll call you later. This isn't the place." Flashing a grin at the receptionist, he slid his phone in his pocket, then stepped outside where the countertop was being loaded into the bed of his truck. If the woman inside was anything like his grandmother, his phone conversation would be the talk of the town.

Back at Tatym's place, he whistled for Ebony. The dog usually met him the second he pulled up. Not wanting her locked up all day, Tatym said the dog would be fine up there without another house around for miles. He'd agreed until now. Dane whistled again, louder and shriller.

His heart rate returned to normal when the dog bounded from the trees with something dangling from her mouth. "Drop it, girl."

Dane jumped back as a snake stretched to its full length of three feet and slithered away from them. "You're lucky that's a rat snake. No snake hunting. Hear me?" He ruffled the fur on the dog's head. "Come keep me company until your human returns."

He slid the countertop free of its cardboard protection and carried it into the house. The concrete would look great against the black and white glass-tiled backsplash. Tatym definitely had good decorating taste. Maybe she'd help him once he purchased a place of his own.

By the time she returned from work, he'd installed the countertop. All he had left to do before he was no longer needed was to replace the cabinets. The thought saddened him. He liked it up here where peace filled the air, at least most the time. Dane wanted such a place.

"Breakfast for supper?" Tatym held up a bag. "Chocolate gravy and biscuits."

"Right up my alley." He held the door open for her and presented the counter with a flourishing sweep of his arm.

"It's gorgeous." Tatym set the bag on the table and ran her hand across the counter's surface. "You're almost finished here."

She sounded almost sad, or maybe it was wishful thinking. "I have a feeling I'll finish before we put to rest the intruder situation."

"Then what? You'll be bored up here with nothing to do."

"I'll find another job. That's what independent contractors do." Time to start advertising harder than he had been. "My grandmother has some things that need fixing." He needed a job that offered more than free rent.

"You'll find something. Once you post pictures online of what you've done here, you'll have to hire someone to help you." She smiled and scraped the gravy into a microwaveable bowl.

"You're in a good mood."

"Easy day at work, and I came up with an idea." She set the bowl in the microwave and pushed a couple of buttons.

"Such as?" He arched a brow.

"How to make our intruder face me." She squared her shoulders and turned to face him. "If it doesn't work, we can safely say he is no longer a threat, and you can return home."

He wasn't going to like this. "Details, please?"

"I'm going to start digging."

~

He couldn't tell if Dane was lying or not. After taking his family to breakfast at the diner, he'd sat in his truck and thought about what the man had said. Which was very little.

What if his grandmother was senile? No, Dane had hinted about the deed without giving anything away. If someone found the deed before he did, he'd have no proof the land didn't belong to Tatym.

His tires squealed driving away from his house. Work beckoned and missing too much would arouse suspicion. The last thing he needed was someone calling Becky to see if everything was all right.

He'd killed the old woman a month ago and was no closer to his goal than he was then. A stubborn young woman, a strong young man…both of whom could easily find the deed before he did. They lived up there. Everything would be for naught. He pounded the steering wheel. What he needed was more time to search, more time to frighten Tatym away, more time to remove Dane from the picture.

~

The next morning, Tatym stood at the top of the cliff, coffee in hand, and waited for the sun to rise. It didn't take long for Dane to join her.

"I wanted to yesterday but overslept," he said.

"Shh." Tatym took a sip of her coffee. Talking would spoil the magic of the sun and mist. She needed the quiet to figure out how she felt about Dane spending this precious time with her. Realizing he might be leaving her soon made her happy and sad at the same time. Happy that she'd have her independence back, but sad because she really did enjoy his company. His presence made her feel safe even with her stubborn resolve to take matters into her own hands.

The sun rose making the mist sparkle before slowly burning it away to reveal the valley below. Tatym sighed and closed her eyes, lifting her face to the sun, before facing Dane. He seemed to be as enthralled as she was.

"It's beautiful," he said softly.

"A sight I'll never grow tired of seeing every morning."

Time to start digging. While she hated putting holes in her yard, she wanted the man to see evidence of her search. She'd keep the digging to the perimeter and hope for the best. What if the deed existed and she found it? She could lose this place. Tatum returned her cup to the sink, then headed out the back door to the garage and grabbed a shovel.

Dane lounged in the doorway. "You're serious?"

"Absolutely. If you're trying to lure him out, so am I. You'll be leaving soon, and I need to know I'll be okay up here with just Ebony."

"Do you know how to shoot a gun?"

"I haven't shot one since I was in junior high."

Which meant she most likely wouldn't be much good.

"I'll go get mine. We can practice when you're tired of digging holes."

"Okay." Tatym slung the shovel over her shoulder and set off toward the trees, Ebony padding along beside her. She'd thought of purchasing a gun after the brazen act of the man circling her house under the motion lights.

While Dane headed down the mountain, she started digging. It was a crazy thing to do and a huge waste of her day off, but ten holes wouldn't take too long and might send the message she wanted to send. That if a deed existed, she intended to be the one to find it.

Digging turned out to be almost therapeutic. Tatym was surprised to find out almost two hours had passed since Dane left. She'd meant to only dig for an hour and work on her garden for whatever time she had left. Tatym leaned the shovel against the wall of the house and went inside to wash her hands. When she returned outside, Dane stood there, having set up a target near the holes she'd dug opposite the house.

"I brought a rifle and a handgun. You might as well practice with both." He jerked his head to the back deck.

The guns lay on the outside table. "I'd like to purchase both and go hunting. Fishing, too. Best way to eat organic."

"I like venison as much as anyone else, but you sure think a lot about healthy eating." He shook his head. "Give me a big, greasy burger."

"A heart attack waiting to happen."

"At least I'd die happy." He laughed. "Come on. For the rifle, I brought you a beanbag to rest the barrel on. You'll need to learn to shoot without it, but we'll start here. It's a 243. My grandmother's gun. If you like it, she'll sell it to you for a hundred."

"Seems fair."

After an hour of shooting, turned out she was quite good, so she suggested they stop for lunch. "I'm satisfied with my progress. The handgun isn't as accurate as the rifle, but if someone comes for me, I doubt I'll have time for anything but the smaller weapon." Besides, her shoulder and wrist hurt. She needed a break.

"You did great. If you want to, we can go to the pawn shop in town and find you a handgun. Do you want the rifle?"

"Yes. Tell your grandmother thank you for me. Sandwich okay?"

"Fine with me."

She left him to clean up while she went to prepare a late lunch of ham and Swiss sandwiches and BBQ-flavored chips. Two glasses of sweet tea, and things were ready. Why hadn't Dane come inside?

She stepped onto the deck. No sight of Dane or Ebony, and the white target still stood where it had been placed. She glanced at the table. The handgun was gone.

Throat dry, she left the deck, her eyes darting each way and her ears alert for signs of where Dane and her dog had gone. Not hearing anything, she headed for the trees, taking the rifle and a handful of ammo with her.

Not wanting to barge through the brush like an enraged bear, she kept her pace slow so she could hear. Her gaze swept back and forth. She found a footprint but couldn't tell if it had been made recently. They hadn't had rain in a few days, so most likely no new prints would be made. Oh, she wasn't a tracker by any stretch of the imagination.

A bark sounded to her right. Tatym moved faster as

a second bark sounded. She froze at the sound of crashing through the brush, then relaxed at the sight of Ebony.

"What is it?"

Her dog barked again and looked back the way she'd come.

"Lead the way." Since she'd returned without Dane, Tatym feared the worst.

Ebony led her to where Dane lay on a game trail, his eyes shut. This was the same trail the intruder liked to travel.

With a wail, Tatym dropped to her knees and felt for a pulse. Steady and strong. Thank you, Lord. Dane's handgun lay in the leaves beside him, a thick branch behind him. That answered the question of whether her intruder had left. Who else would knock Dane unconscious and leave the gun?

Where was her phone? Could she leave him here while she called the sheriff and 911 for an ambulance? The danger for both of them was escalating.

Chapter Ten

Tatym raced back to the cabin, ordering Ebony to stay with Dane, and snatched her phone from the table. Seconds later, she placed the two calls. On her way back to him, Dane came stumbling toward her. "You shouldn't be up. I've called the sheriff and an ambulance." She rushed to his side and propped her shoulder under his.

"I'll be fine."

"You were unconscious. Where's your gun?" She felt around his waist.

"Back there, I reckon."

"Stay here." She helped him sit under a tree and darted to where he'd been lying. Thankfully, his gun still nestled on a pile of dry leaves.

Dane still sat where she'd left him, head back and eyes closed. "I feel dead. Am I? My head is killing me."

"You wouldn't feel anything if you were dead. Let's stay put and wait for the ambulance. You shouldn't be walking around."

"Okay." He laid on his back in the grass and stared at the sky, Ebony plopping down beside him. "Come." He patted the ground on the other side of him.

"Did you see who hit you?" She lowered to the grass

and mimicked his posture. Lying there in the grass, she gazed up at the indigo sky sprinkled with stars. At any other time, it would signify the most romantic moment in her life. Romantic?

"Shh." He took her hand in his. "No, I didn't. Let's not spoil this…with talk of rotten things."

So, he felt it too—the sweetness that hung in the air in that second of time, despite Dane's attack.

She tilted her head to look at him. As if sensing her eyes on him, Dane met her gaze. The hand not holding hers caressed her check, the back of his hands as soft as silk.

"You look as if you're made out of porcelain." The hand stopped and cupped the back of her head. "I'm going to kiss you to make sure you're real."

"You're out of it, Dane," she whispered, leaning forward despite her mind shouting no. Dane might not remember the kiss by morning, but she would. Might as well seize the opportunity. Her gaze fell on his chiseled lips as they descended on hers.

A kiss so tender it brought tears to her eyes and was way too short. Then Dane groaned and fell back, unconscious.

Tatym put her ear to his chest. Thank you, God. A strong heartbeat. Emergency lights flashed through the trees, so she pushed to her feet to greet them. The sheriff's car pulled up behind the ambulance. Two medics and Sheriff Westbrook followed Tatym to Dane.

His eyes flickered open as the two paramedics lifted him onto a gurney. "I'm fine."

"He isn't. This is the second time being unconscious."

"I'll drive you to the hospital in my car," the sheriff

said to her. "Then I'm going to want to ask Dane some questions when he's coherent."

"Okay." She put the dog in the house and hurried to the passenger side door as Dane was carried into the ambulance.

They made it to the small hospital in Misty Hollow in silence. Tatym didn't want small talk. Thankfully, the sheriff wasn't a talkative man.

After an hour or so, the nurse permitted them to go to Dane's room, where he now sat up in a bed.

"How are you feeling?" She noted the crease between his eyes.

"Headache, but they're bringing me something." He closed his eyes. "Ask your questions, Sheriff."

"Can't it wait a bit? At least until he takes a pain pill?" Tatym sat in a hard plastic chair against the wall.

"Since I didn't see who hit me, I can't tell you anything about the person. They hit me from behind." Dane kept his eyes closed.

"Why did you leave the yard?" Tatym asked. "You were there one minute and gone the next."

"Ebony growled toward the trees. I caught sight of what I thought looked like a person standing in the shadows. So, we gave chase. Somehow, he came up behind me. That's all I remember."

She piped in. "When I first noticed him missing, I grabbed my gun and—"

"Hold on." The sheriff glanced up from where he wrote Dane's statement on a legal pad of paper. "You had a gun?"

"Yes. Dane taught me to shoot today. Well, I already knew how, but it had been—"

"Back to the story please." Sheriff Westbrook shook

his head. "Get a permit."

"Right. After I went maybe a quarter of a mile into the woods, I heard Ebony bark. Then, I found Dane on the ground. The intruder is back."

The sheriff nodded. "We've been checking into anyone who might have been out of town during the time you weren't bothered. No one fits. But, the intruder always comes through the woods, so there's no reason to think it wasn't him." He stood. "If you do remember anything, let me know. I'll send a car to take you home, Tatym. Be careful. Don't go anywhere alone."

"Thank you." She wouldn't need to. Hopefully, the man in the woods would have seen her holes and figured she was searching for the deed with Dane. He'd have to make a move then. Plus, she'd decided to stay in Dane's hospital room until she felt certain he really was going to be okay.

~

He punched a hole in the wall of the garage with his fist. They were both looking for what belonged to him.

"Sweetheart?" His wife stepped out of the house. "Something wrong?"

"Rough day." He rubbed his fist. "I'll fix the hole this weekend."

"That's not important right now. What is important is what's bothering you." She crossed her arms. "You've been out of sorts for weeks now. Won't you tell me what's on your mind?"

He'd love to, but until he could prove the land was theirs, he couldn't risk her reaction. His sweet Becky had strong principles. "Too much work, not enough time."

"You need to set boundaries with your clients, honey, or you'll work yourself into an early grave. Why not cut out the evening jobs? You aren't sleeping enough."

He gave her a peck on the check as he entered the house. "You worry too much. But, I'm home early enough tonight. The boys still up?"

"They're putting their pajamas on." She followed him inside and closed the door behind her. "Please consider staying home in the evenings. We miss you."

He could and slip out after his wife went to sleep, but that would cut into his sleeping time even further. There had to be a way to fulfill his quest and keep his family happy at the same time. It would come to him.

It had felt wonderful, powerful, to sneak up on the cowboy and knock him down. For a middle-aged man, he'd done quite well. The pride he felt for hitting Dane helped soothe the anger for having competition.

Things needed to escalate, become more dangerous to Tatym for resisting. He didn't want to kill again, but he would if he had to.

~

Dane had a bad concussion according to the doctor. Since he refused to let Tatym return to the cabin alone, he denied the doctor's request to spend the night in the hospital. He could sleep just as well at home. *Home.* Wow. How quickly he'd started thinking of the cabin in that way.

"I don't think you should leave. I'll sleep in the chair," Tatym told him. "What if you go to sleep and don't wake up?"

"The danger of that is past." He glanced at the doctor who gave a reluctant nod.

"Other than a headache and dizziness, he should be fine," the doctor said. "I'll release you, but you have to promise to take it easy for the next three days."

"It's a deal." Three days of not working prolonged his time at the cabin with Tatym.

"That means no driving."

He scowled. How could he follow Tatym back and forth to work if he couldn't drive? She didn't work the early shift, so that wasn't a problem. He'd feel fine by the next day, surely. He'd figure it out. "Okay, fine."

Half an hour later, he sat in the front passenger seat of a paid driver's car, Misty Hollow's version of a taxi, leaving the back seat for Tatym who dozed off ten minutes into the thirty-minute drive. Dane didn't blame her. He could sleep for hours.

Back at the cabin, Ebony barked from inside. Poor thing. It had been hours since she'd been out.

"Wake up, sweetheart." He paid the driver and opened the back door, holding out a hand to a drowsy Tatym.

"I should be helping you."

"I'm steady enough."

"Go on in. I'll stay out here until Ebony is done." She fished the house key from the pocket of her jeans.

"I'll sit on the porch." He let the dog out and slowly lowered himself to the top step.

Ebony trotted in circles, did her business, and returned to the house.

She yawned. "Thank goodness. I feel as if I could sleep for a week. I'm glad I don't go to work until ten. That gives me enough sleep."

Dane nodded. She'd get seven hours if she went to sleep right away.

"Leave your door open," she said. "I want to be able to hear you if you need me."

If he died in his sleep, he wouldn't be able to call for her. "All right." He smiled and locked the door behind him before checking all the windows and heading to his room.

Something moving around overhead woke him shortly after dawn. At first, he thought he dreamed the sound, but Tatym stood in the doorway of his room.

"There's something in the attic."

That had him shooting from bed. He grabbed the bedpost until the dizziness passed, then moved to the living room. "It doesn't sound like a critter," he whispered. The footsteps were too heavy. That meant a human was walking around in the attic.

Ebony stared upward and growled, then broke into a frenzied barking.

"Here." Tatym thrust his gun into his hands. "Be careful."

He nodded and reached for the rope that lowered the trapdoor. As it opened, he carefully pulled down the ladder.

Footsteps pounded overhead.

"Outside." Tatym darted for the door.

Dane scrambled up the ladder in time to see a slightly heavyset man wearing a ski mask climb out the window. Dark eyes glittered through the eye holes.

He knew this man—at least he recognized his build. He'd seen him before, but the bulky clothes and mask hid his identity.

"You should stop right there." Dane aimed his weapon.

The man moved out of sight.

A gunshot rang out, then another.

Ebony yelped, then barked ferociously.

"Stay, girl!" Tatym's order rang through the window from outside.

Dane leaned out as the man dashed for the woods, followed by Tatum, but he had too much of a lead for a handgun to reach. "No, Tatym."

She stopped her chase. "I can catch him."

"He'll shoot you. Come back inside."

How long had the man been up there? Had he watched them sleep? Stared at Tatym in her bed? No, the dog would have alerted them. They'd all been too tired to hear anything until that morning.

He closed and locked the window, then joined Tatym in the living room. "Please, don't chase after bad guys by yourself again. Is the dog okay?"

She nodded. "He shot at her but missed. By the time I got my gun up, he was too far away. Next time, I'll take the rifle."

He hoped there wouldn't be a next time, but the guy grew bolder. How long until one of them was killed? "We'd be better off staying with my grandmother."

Chapter Eleven

They ought to get the idea now. The whack against Dane's head should have sent a message they'd understand. Now, he needed to return home before Becky started to worry.

She was waiting up for him on the sofa in the living room, mad as a wet hen. "I can't do this anymore, Frank, and I want an honest answer. Are you having an affair? Why are you dressed all in black? Is that a ski mask hanging from your pocket?"

Drat. He'd forgotten to put the mask in his glove compartment. "Sweetheart, of course I'm not having an affair. I'm just really busy with work."

"Too busy. You're neglecting me and the boys. Taking us to the diner once a week does not fulfill your father and husband duties." She crossed her arms. "Something has to change or I'm taking the boys to my parents."

His blood boiled, and his hands curled into fists. "Everything I do is for you and the boys. How dare you threaten me with leaving."

She took a step back, fear flickering in her eyes. "We need you around more. Your absence affects your son's diabetes. You've changed, Frank. It's like I don't even know the man I'm married to."

"Don't be ridiculous." He didn't need this drama. She'd be sorry if she left. He wouldn't give her a cent of his future fortune if she did. "Now go to bed. I have another busy day tomorrow." Ignoring the other questions, he stormed past her and up the stairs.

~

Tatym folded her arms over her chest like a shield. "If we leave, this guy wins."

"If he manages to kill one of us, he wins." Dane lowered to the sofa.

She plopped in the chair across from him. What Dane said was true, but if they left, the man would have complete access to her land. "Leaving won't stop him from trying to drive me away. He wants the alleged deed. This land will not pass from my hands unless I'm dead or sell." She didn't plan on either of those options.

"God spare me stubborn women." He slowly rose to his feet and returned to his room.

Tatym didn't enjoy being obstinate, but running away wouldn't end this. Staying put and continuing with the ruse of looking for the deed would. She leaned against the back of the chair.

Eventually, they'd have to say they'd found what they were looking for. Could it be possible to modify the original? Make a copy that looked a hundred years old and pass it off as real? "I need to go to the bank and get the deed from the safety deposit box."

Dane, now dressed, exited his room with a briefcase. "Why?"

She explained her idea. "Do you think it will work?"

"Maybe." He shrugged. "If we can find someone talented enough to age the document."

"I'd better be on my way then. I work at ten, and the bank opens at nine. I can grab breakfast at the diner."

"Sounds like a plan to me. I could go for some steak and eggs."

She frowned. "The doctor said you need to take it easy for a few days."

"A man still needs to eat. Sitting in a booth isn't going to hurt me."

And he called her stubborn? Shaking her head, she went to her room to put on her uniform. She slipped the safety deposit-box key into the pocket of the dress. This plan would work. It had to. Before either she or Dane was killed.

The bank manager, Kelly Turner, greeted them with a smile. "The last time that box was opened was when your grandmother was here and someone else was the manager."

"Kingsley." Dane nodded. "I hope you aren't working with the mob."

She laughed. "Definitely not. Follow me, Miss Billings."

Tatym shot Dane a look, then followed the woman. She wouldn't have minded him coming, but since he didn't ask, she let it be.

The manager used her key, then stepped back for Tatym to use hers. "Call me when you're finished. I'll be right outside the door."

"Thank you." Tatym unlocked the box and pulled it out to set on a table. She took a deep breath and opened the box.

Inside lay the deed to the house which she slipped into her pocket, a copy of Grandma's will, and a letter. Tatym opened the letter and read:

Dear Tatym,

Don't believe the rumors. The cabin and the land it sits on has been in our family for over a hundred years purchased from the Olsons in the 1800s. I fear I'm not long for this world due to my refusal to be run off. A lot of suspicious activity happening. I suspect the same may happen to you, and for that I apologize. Keep your wits about you. Stay strong. Believe that God's will prevails.

Remember you are loved, you are strong, and you will figure out what I could not.

Your grandmother.

Tatym swiped the back of her hand across her face to wipe away the tears that had fallen. As far as she was concerned, this was the final proof her grandmother's death was at the hands of another. Someone who had access to insulin and could get close to her grandmother.

She replaced the box and knocked on the door for the manager to secure the will. The deed and the letter would leave with Tatym.

In her car, she handed the letter to Dane and drove to the diner. When he'd finished, he handed it back. "I wish the sheriff could've helped stop this in time."

Tatym nodded. "I'm sure he would have tried his best if he'd suspected anything." The man was former FBI after all. "Are you going to sit in the diner until I'm off work?" She cut him a sideways glance. "You shouldn't be driving."

"I brought my laptop to finish some work. I'll also

check on my grandmother and pick up some things from the hardware store—I can walk to all those places. Then I'll stop by the sheriff's office and let him know about this morning and this letter. I'll fill you in on anything I find out when your shift is over."

Tatym wished she could visit the sheriff with him, but she needed her job, too. She might as well use Dane to help her get to the bottom of who was bothering her. He was willing enough, and she enjoyed having him around.

He made her feel protected. Maybe too protected. Having him around might be the only reason she felt safe enough to stay at the cabin.

~

Since they arrived at the diner a half an hour before her shift started, Dane ordered steak and eggs while Tatym ordered a ham-and-cheese omelet. His mind raced with the escalating danger, and he needed to take Tatym away from Misty Hollow to somewhere safe.

"Why isn't this guy deterred by the lights and cameras?" She tilted her head. "Is he that confident we won't discover his identity?"

"Maybe." Dane poured creamer into his coffee. "I feel as if I know him. There is something familiar about his build, his eyes."

"Hopefully you'll figure it out soon." She gobbled down her breakfast and excused herself. "Be careful. Try to rest at your grandmother's. You're still injured."

"I'm sure once she finds out about my concussion, she'll nag me until I lie down for a bit."

"Good." She grinned and cleared the table. "Give me a wave if you want more coffee."

"I will." He opened his laptop and spent the next

hour making fliers, putting an ad in the local newspaper and online, and searching for someone in town that might be able to age the cabin's deed which turned out to be harder than he'd thought. What he needed was a graphic-design student.

He waved the hostess over and explained what he needed. "Do you know of anyone?"

"I'd ask at the high school if I were you. I bet one of the students in the computer class could help."

"That's a good idea. Thanks." He closed his laptop and put everything back in his briefcase. Time to visit the sheriff.

Sheriff Westbrook's brow lowered. "In her attic? That's too close."

"Who around town uses insulin?"

"I'm sure there are a few. I'll send someone to speak to the pharmacist." He folded his hands on the top of his desk. "Tatym needs to stay in town until we catch this guy."

"She won't. I've tried. Instead, she came up with another idea. One that might work but will also increase the danger." He told about aging the deed. "I'm headed to the high school when I leave here."

"I don't like it. This man is growing desperate. You might get more than a knock on the head for your trouble. Oh, and your grandmother is spitting mad. One of the nurses told her about you having a concussion." He grinned. "She said she should have heard it from you first. If I were you, I'd go see her before going to the school."

"Agreed." Dane stood, mentally preparing himself for a tongue-lashing. He'd have time to be lectured and still reach the school before classes let out.

Like a teenager sneaking in after curfew, he opened the front door of his grandmother's house as quietly as possible. Grandma, seated at the kitchen table, cleared her throat, her hands twirling an empty coffee cup. Dane gave a long exhale.

"I'm sorry. I should have called you, but I didn't want to worry you." He sat in the chair across from her.

"Would I have felt better getting the call that you'd been murdered?" She arched a brow. "A concussion is nothing compared to that, but as your grandmother, I deserved a call. It's embarrassing to hear the news from someone who expected me already to know."

He felt like the worst grandson in the world. "You have a right to be upset." When no response was forthcoming, he changed tactics. "Would you like to hear the latest on Tatym's property?" Maybe a change of subject would soothe her ruffled feathers.

"I'm listening." She crossed her arms.

He told her about being hit, the letter in the safety-deposit box, and Tatym's plans to draw the suspect into the open. "I tried to persuade her to come here where it's safer, but she declined."

"Of course, she did. She's like her grandmother. Tough. Strong. She won't run, which means you'll be in constant danger around her. Have you noticed that every time a new girl comes to town, death follows?"

He laughed. "Coincidence." Eerily correct, though. Now, he wondered why they rarely had new men come to town.

She wagged her finger at him. "I don't believe in coincidence. New girls arrive, they fall in love, people die. In the last year or so, it's happened to four women before Tatym. That mist everyone loves keeps this town living on the dark side."

"You've lost your mind." He shook his head. "Do I need to worry about your mental state?"

"Don't sass me, young man."

He reached across and patted her hand. "I don't need to pick Tatym up until seven. What would you like me to do for you?"

"Take a nap. You're injured, remember?"

Yes, his head ached. A nap sounded wonderful. "Wake me in an hour, then I'll do a chore that needs doing before heading to the high school."

"You'll stay for lunch, then go." She planted her hands flat on the table and pushed to her feet. "I'll wake you in an hour."

Dane climbed the stairs, surprised to see fresh sheets on the bed. Did his grandmother keep them fresh on the off chance it was the night he'd come home? He hoped not because the danger to Tatym wouldn't be going away any time soon. And Dane would stay with her until it was over.

Chapter Twelve

Dane sat in the principal's office—a place he'd once frequented a lot. At least he was no longer that unruly kid.

"Good afternoon." Mr. White entered the office and took a seat at his desk. "Sorry to keep you waiting."

"It's not a problem. I'm looking for someone good with graphic design, really good, and someone who can keep a secret. The sheriff suggested one of your tech students."

The principal steepled his fingers under his chin. "No one comes to mind. Let's visit the lab. The teacher, Mr. Roy, will know." He stood.

Dane followed him to the second floor and into a roomful of laptops. The clicking of fingers on keyboards filled the air.

The teacher, a young man who looked fresh out of college, approached them. "Can I help you?"

"We hope so. Let's step outside." Mr. White motioned his head toward the door.

"Remember, class, I can see you through the window." The teacher followed them out.

"I have a document that I'd like to be aged but authentic-looking. The sheriff thought one of your students might be able to do so. They would also have to be discreet. I need it to look a hundred years old."

Mr. Roy twisted his lips. "It's tricky making modern fonts look old. It'd be best if you paid someone to write in shorthand on aged parchment paper."

The man had a point. "Know of anyone who can do that?"

"I can. I have good handwriting. If you aren't happy with the result, don't pay me. If you are happy, how's a hundred dollars?"

"Sounds fair." Dane handed him a photocopy of Tatym's deed. "Remember not to say anything to anyone. I'll let the sheriff know you have this." If Mr. Roy believed it to be a law-enforcement matter, he might be less likely to have loose lips. "Thank you. Any idea how long it will take?"

"A couple of nights. I'll let the sheriff know when it's finished."

Dane smiled. He liked having the sheriff as the middleman. It might make the suspect less suspicious.

He thanked both men and hurried from the school as the release bell rang. He didn't relish being stuck in after-school traffic. Back in Tatym's car, he drove to the diner, prepared to spend the last few hours of her shift doing paperwork for his business.

Tatym glanced over while carrying a large tray of plates to a table.

Dane took a seat in a far booth and opened his laptop. She'd come over to see what he'd done that day when she had the chance.

Tatym had a break a half an hour later and slid into the booth across from him, setting a glass of soda on the table. "Well?"

"The plan's chugging right along." He lowered his voice and explained what the high school teacher suggested they do. "Mr. Roy made a good point about computer fonts not looking authentic."

"That is good news. I didn't think of that." She took a sip of her drink. "Once we have the fake, we show it around and voilà. Bad guy behind bars."

If only it could be that easy. "Let's hope so, anyway."

"When you've finished with your fliers, I bet Lucy will let you post one in the window. I've seen other advertisements there." She slid from the booth. "Are you sticking around until quitting time?"

"Yes. Could you bring me whatever the special is? It's suppertime." He flashed a grin.

"It's always suppertime for you. How's the head?"

"Just a dull ache. It'll be even better tomorrow, and as promised I took a nap."

She smiled. "Good boy."

~

"You seem to be a million miles away," Heather said after seating the Grayson family in a booth. "Not to mention how you've stared at every man who entered the diner today. What's up? I wouldn't think you'd be interested in anyone else with the handsome Dane following you around."

Tatym glanced around to make sure no one paid them too much attention. "I'm convinced that whoever is trying to scare me away and hit Dane frequents the diner. I see a few men who match the body type of the man I saw, but I can't be sure which one could be him."

"You'll drive yourself crazy trying to figure that

out. Let the sheriff's department handle things."

"They don't have any leads so far." Tatym gripped her order pad and headed for the Graysons' table. "Have you decided?"

"The boys will have chicken strips and fries," Mrs. Grayson said. "I'll have the chef salad. Frank?"

"Mushroom burger."

Tatym gathered the menus. "Drinks?" Once she had what they wanted, she sent in their order to the kitchen.

Lucy turned from the stove where she flipped burgers. "Let folks know their orders will take longer. The chef left sick, and I'm running behind."

"Anything I can do to help?"

"Keep the diners as happy as possible and offer my apologies." She returned her attention to the stove.

Because of the slow turnaround from order to delivery, Tatym didn't leave work until almost eight. Dane remained patient, even taking a small nap in the booth he occupied. She gently shook him awake.

"I'm sorry it's so late."

"No worries. I finished a lot of work I've been pushing aside." He closed his laptop and slid it and some papers into his briefcase before tossing her the keys to her truck.

Tatym chuckled. She hadn't liked the fact he drove around town that day. A concussion was a serious matter. But, he needed to do the legwork since she had to work.

A vehicle pulled from a side road as she started the drive up the mountain. At first, she didn't think it anything unusual until it followed so close the lights reflected off her rearview mirror, blinding her. "There's a jerk right on our tail."

Dane turned in his seat. "Pull over and let them pass

at the first opportunity."

There were few places on the curvy road for a car to pass and even fewer where one could pull off. If Tatym slowed, the vehicle behind them would hit them. Was that their intent or did they merely want to intimidate? Tatym wished now that she'd let Dane drive. She clutched the steering wheel so tight her knuckles ached.

The drive had never taken longer.

"Do you have your gun?" Dane asked, his gaze still on the vehicle behind them.

"No. I left it at home. You?"

"It's in my truck. We need to be better about keeping them on us."

She shot him a quick glance. "You think we need them right now?"

"I don't know, but I have a bad feeling."

Which made her anxiety shoot up. Tatym pressed the accelerator, willing to take a chance on increasing her speed. She doubted she'd meet anyone coming down the mountain. No one lived any further up but her. Which meant whoever was behind them was following.

Her mother had always told her not to go home if she felt as if she were being followed. She didn't have a choice this time.

An orange glow in the sky drew her attention. "Dane. Look. Something's on fire." Please, God, not the cabin."

The vehicle behind them stopped and backed away with a short tap of its horn.

Her head pounded as she rounded the last curve.

Flames shot up from behind the house. "Call the fire department!" She shoved open her door. "Ebony?"

The dog barged from the doggy door and ran to her

side, her body trembling. She licked Tatym's hand and whined.

"I'd love to give you a hug, but there's work to do." She darted for the faucet on the back of the house and grabbed the water hose. It would take a while for the fire department to arrive, and her garage was up in flames.

"Wait." Dane unhooked the hose and inserted a Y link before adding another hose. "This is too big for one."

She aimed her hose on one side of the garage, Dane the other. They fought a losing battle. The fire was too big, but still they had to try.

The roof groaned and collapsed minutes before the fire department arrived. Tatym's shoulders sagged.

Dane shut off the water and gathered her into his arms. "At least it wasn't the house."

She leaned into him. "It will be next time. I need to hire a security guard to be here when we aren't."

"I know of a retired policeman who might be willing." He sighed. "The sheriff's here."

"Did you call him?" She raised her head as Sheriff Westbrook jumped out of his car.

"No."

They turned to greet him.

"I was headed home when the call came across the scanner. Since you've been having trouble, I decided to come have a look for myself and talk to the fire chief."

The sheriff suspected foul play without even seeing the garage. Tatym did, too. "I kept a couple of cans of gasoline in the garage."

"No explosion?"

She shook her head. "I bet the gas was used to start the fire."

"We'll find out soon enough."

With Dane's arm around her waist, they watched the fire department put out the fire. Tatym couldn't wait to face the man causing her trouble. She wasn't prone to violence, but she'd derive great satisfaction with a well-placed punch to the face.

"I'll check the camera footage." A few minutes later, she showed the sheriff video of the man setting the fire.

~

He'd thought about running them off the road after setting the fire and driving to the other side of the mountain. But, he'd been sent on an errand, and Becky vowed to be gone if he stayed out too late again.

That made twice she'd threatened him. If it happened again, he'd help her pack. No one threatened him when everything he did was for his family. She'd regret her attitude once he became rich.

He pulled into the driveway and grabbed the bag of milk and bread from the passenger seat. At least it was almost time for bed. He wouldn't have to make small talk for long.

"Why do you smell like gasoline?" Becky wrinkled her nose.

"Had to fill my tank and wasn't paying attention. Some dripped on my shoe." Nosy woman. He set the bag on the table. "Store was crowded at this late hour. Next time you do the weekly shopping, buy extra bread and milk."

She frowned. "Sorry I asked you. Next time, you can stay home with the kids."

"I didn't mean to come across as harsh." Staying home wouldn't give him the time he needed, and he was so close to running Tatym off her land.

Following her, then the fire…yes, she was sure to be on the brink of letting it all go.

He had no qualms about upping the danger if she didn't. He'd done the same with her grandmother, Alice had confronted him with her suspicions, and he had to jab her with the insulin he'd just picked up from the pharmacist for his son. Then, another jab for good measure. He'd lied to Becky and told her the pharmacy had run out and would replace it in a few days. It had cost him a pretty penny, too, because insurance wouldn't pay.

He was so deep in his thoughts he didn't realized Becky had asked him a question. "Sorry?"

She exhaled heavily. "I asked what you thought about the information that Tatym Billings and Dane James may have found the other deed to her land."

"Not *her* land unless that original deed says so." Which it didn't. "You know some believe the Billings stole that land."

She scoffed. "Ridiculous. My grandfather once told me it has belonged to the Billings family for over a century."

Frank whipped around to face her. "Shut your lying mouth before I shut it for you."

She recoiled. "Frank!"

Rubbing both hands briskly down his face, he shook his head. "I'm sorry. I'm not feeling well. Forgive me." He headed for the bedroom. The stress was making his whole body ache. He needed to end this quickly.

Chapter Thirteen

After a restless night, Tatym climbed out of bed. Worry about her cabin burning down had kept her awake. Hopefully, the man Dane knew would be able to guard the place during the day.

Tatym booted up her laptop at the kitchen table. No activity occurred after the man in a ski mask had set fire to the garage. She really hoped the guy making the fake deed was quick. They needed this to end before she lost everything. All she had was on top of this mountain. Grandma's truck, the cabin, the land, Ebony, and…Dane. He'd come to mean a lot to her since working on the cabin. She'd miss him very much when this was over.

"Good morning." Dane, tousled hair and bare-chested, stood in the doorway. "You're up early."

"Couldn't sleep." She smiled up at him. Did he realize how seeing him half-dressed affected her? He didn't seem to. Nothing improper in his stance or his gaze. She stood. "I'll make coffee for us to sip while we watch the sun rise."

"Perfect. I'll get dressed."

Thank goodness. She measured the coffee grounds and started the percolator. It wasn't what she was used to, but she didn't want to replace something her grandmother had enjoyed.

By the time Dane returned, his hair now wet from a shower, the coffee was done. She handed him a cup. "At least there's still the sunrise."

He put a hand on her shoulder. "I'll start rebuilding the garage tomorrow. Today, I'll talk to the ex-cop and purchase supplies. You can pay me back when the insurance money comes in."

"That might take a while."

"It's fine." He smiled. "We'll be okay."

She held onto that hope and headed for the front door. Before stepping onto the porch, she looked around the area. No unpleasant surprises.

A full moon cast light over everything. The first full moon since she'd arrived, and it made the view of the mist more magical than before. Silvery, the mist shimmered like fine silk. At least the arsonist couldn't burn this away. Only the sun could dispel the mist which would arrive again like the promise of a rainbow after a storm.

By now Dane knew to remain silent as the sun made its appearance. Could there be anything more perfect than enjoying such a view with a good man, a sweet dog, and a cup of coffee?

"Beautiful," Dane whispered, except he wasn't watching the view.

Tatym turned and stared into his eyes. Without making a conscious effort to do so, she leaned in.

His lips met hers as the sun kissed away the mist. Yes, there was something better than the view. Kissing Dane on top of that cliff as the sun rose.

When they were both breathless, Dane leaned his

forehead against hers. "I think I'll do that every morning I'm here."

A nervous giggle escaped her. "That sounds like a wonderful idea." Just like that, everything changed between them. They were no longer woman and hired hand but something much more.

"I have the morning shift today. Let me buy you breakfast." She stepped back.

"You know I never turn down food."

"Yes, I do." She laughed and turned toward the house.

Dane grabbed her hand and pulled her back for a quick kiss. "Now, you can go."

Her skin warm and her smile wide, Tatym practically floated into the house. His kiss almost made her forget about the deed and the danger until they climbed in Dane's truck. Then the night before came flooding back. The drive down the mountain was tense, as she expected to be followed and driven off the road.

When they arrived safely at the diner, she released the breath she'd held onto and let go of the grip handle above her head. She thought about Dane's offer to stay at his grandmother's but brushed the idea aside again. Leaving her land would mean the other guy won. Foolhardy, yes, but if her grandmother refused to leave, so would she. At least, Tatym was more aware of the danger than her grandmother had been, which meant she might be the victor this time. Or, she'd be killed. Either way, she wouldn't give up.

She led Dane to the booth in the corner he seemed to prefer and said she'd be back to take his order before heading to the staff lounge behind the kitchen. Chef Rawlings had returned which would make Lucy happy.

Tatym put her purse in her locker and donned her apron, readying herself for another day of work without her discovering the identity of the man who terrorized her. She gave a heavy sigh and slipped a pencil and order pad in her pocket.

"You okay?" Lucy tilted her head.

"I'm exhausted and tired of someone trying to run me off my land." She filled the other woman in on everything that had been happening, leaving out her plans for luring the man into the open.

"Alice was murdered?" Lucy put a hand to her throat. "That breaks my heart. She was my friend."

"You knew her well?"

She nodded. "We'd visit June together quite often. The townspeople sometimes called us the Three Stooges, then Alice died, and June rarely leaves her house. That ended our shenanigans."

"Any idea who might have killed her?"

She shook her head. "Everyone loved Alice."

Apparently not everyone.

~

Dane finished his three-egg omelet, hash browns, and bacon, left a big tip for Tatym, and headed out to find Buster Jones, the ex-police officer. He had an idea where the man's farm was and hoped to see his name on a mailbox.

His phone buzzed before he reached his truck—a text from the sheriff asking him to stop by the office.

The receptionist waved him back as soon as he arrived. "He's waiting for you."

Dane headed down the hall and peered into the sheriff's office. "What's up?"

"Have a seat, please. I've been having my deputies

find out who in town uses insulin. There are quite a few. Without deputizing you, I cannot divulge this information." He folded his hands on his desk. "So, how do you feel about being a deputy for a while? Tatym is in danger and having you with her is the best way to keep her safe. You knowing what is happening with the case will help."

He remembered when his former boss, Liam O'Ryan, had been deputized for a similar reason. While Dane hadn't been privy to any information, he'd seen what it was like second-hand. "I'm willing."

"This will give you some authority. Unless folks start dying, there's no reason for the FBI to become involved. I can use all the help I can get." He opened a drawer and removed a badge.

"But, this is to help protect Tatym, right? Not to be called in on other cases?"

"Correct." He slid the badge across the desk. "Here's the list of people who either use insulin or a family member does. Don't go asking questions; just keep an eye out. See whether any of them seem to be overly interested in Tatym."

The paper held ten names. "Every one of these frequent the diner on a regular basis. At least when I've been there. That's an easy way to keep an eye on Tatym."

"You need to keep an even closer eye on her."

Dane nodded and folded the paper to slide it into his pocket. "Thank you, sir. I'm on my way to see whether Buster Jones will agree to guard the property when we aren't there."

"Good man for the job."

"Do you happen to have an address?"

The sheriff looked it up on his computer, then

scribbled it on a scrap of paper. "Good luck. I'd offer you one of my deputies, but they're needed here."

"Thanks." Dane took his leave and drove to the lowlands outside of town. The GPS on his phone led him to a chicken farm five miles away.

Jones seemed to do well for himself with three chicken houses set at a distance from his house. Surprisingly, the air didn't stink as Dane thought it would.

When knocking at the door didn't bring Jones out, Dane headed for the first chicken house. "Mr. Jones?"

"In here gathering eggs."

Dane followed the sound of his voice.

Jones stood by a conveyor belt where eggs exited a room full of white chickens. "What can I do for you?" He put eggs in a plastic holder.

"I'm Dane James, and I'm looking for someone to guard some property when the owner isn't home. We've had an intruder and an arsonist. I can see you're busy, though."

"Nah, I don't do this every day. I employ a husband and wife who usually do this, but they took the day off." He shut off the belt. "Why me?"

"You're retired law enforcement. Sheriff Westbrook deputized me today." He filled the man in on what had been happening. "I need to focus on Miss Billings, not the cabin and land. We'll pay."

Jones met his gaze, as if sizing Dane up. "I reckon I can. Beats watching TV or mowing the yard. How about fifty bucks each day I sit there? I'm saving for a new truck."

"It's a deal." Dane thrust out his hand. "If you can give me your phone number, I'll call you with the schedule. The view from the mountain is worth the tedium of watching the house, and there's a dog that won't leave your side."

"Sounds better and better." Jones grinned. "I've a dog of my own and would like to bring him with me."

"Feel free." Dane pumped his hand, pleased the man had agreed. One less thing to worry about. He didn't want anything to interfere with him keeping Tatym safe.

~

Things were starting to heat up, and he didn't like the way things were going at home or in his quest to claim the property. Even after apologizing for yelling at Becky, she continued to turn away whenever he came in the room. What had happened to his submissive wife?

Now, he sat in the diner alone listening to the happy conversations around him while keeping an eye on Tatym. With guarded eyes she studied every person who came in.

He wasn't stupid. On the mountain he always padded his clothes and wore a mask. She'd never figure out it was him. Not until they met face-to-face as he and Alice had.

His eyes narrowed as Dane entered the diner and approached Tatym. What was that on his chest? The man had been deputized? Why? Carrying a badge didn't protect the man if he got in the way. But it would effect a harsher sentence for the one who harmed him.

This definitely put a stick in the spoke of his wheel. He slapped money on the table and left before he did something to draw attention to himself. There were a few things on his to-do list before heading home for supper, the boys' yelling, and Becky's sulking.

No matter. He'd pretend to pay attention while

planning his next move. Anything to keep Becky from probing. The last thing he needed was for her to find out what he did when he wasn't home. Better she find out when the deed was done and their bank account full.

Chapter Fourteen

Tatym sat on the front porch nursing her second cup of coffee—something she liked to do on her day off. She and Dane had already watched the sunrise and shared a few kisses. Now, she watched as he gave Mr. Jones a tour around the property.

Before their kiss, she would've taken offense at Dane showing the man around. Now, she sat content and let him take the lead while she stared at the list of possible suspects.

Later, Dane and she would start asking questions about the people on the list by visiting Lucy and his grandmother first. If anyone could point them in the right direction, they could. The sheriff and his deputies were doing the same, but sometimes people were averse to speaking to law enforcement. At least she hoped they'd be more loosely lipped with her and Dane. As long as he didn't flash his badge.

Deputized. She shook her head. Tatym hadn't seen that coming. A few months ago, the sheriff had deputized the rancher Dane had worked for. Moving to Misty Hollow from a larger city left her feeling a bit off-kilter. She wasn't used to local law enforcement being ill-equipped to care for the people it served.

She patted Ebony's head. "We didn't have a visitor last night, girl. Was the fire the last thing he'd do before making his final act?" The thought chilled her blood. His next move could be the death of her. Her resolve to remain at the cabin rather than in town might be the worst decision she'd ever made.

With her coffee having gone cold, Tatym entered the house to get ready to head into town. She wasn't a fan of going to the diner on her day off, but she'd do almost anything to end this danger.

"Tatym, we need to leave. Now." Dane raced through the house and grabbed the keys to his truck. "Fire at my grandmother's house."

What? They'd never reach the house in time. Tatym sprinted after him, shoving the list of suspects into her pocket.

By the time they arrived, the fire was out, and June sat in the ambulance with an oxygen mask over her face. Several townspeople milled around, shock and curiosity on their faces.

"The fire was contained to the sunroom," Sheriff Westbrook said after meeting them. "Your grandmother was sleeping in her bed on the other side of the wall. A little smoke inhalation, but she'll be fine. No damage to the main house. It could have been worse."

"It could have been a lot worse." Dane brushed past the sheriff and rushed to his grandmother.

"Arson?" Tatym peered up at the sheriff.

"We suspect so."

"Dane and I are planning on questioning some of the people on the list you gave him."

"The department is already doing that."

"They might remember something they forgot to tell

you." She tilted her head. "I can't sit still and wait for the man to kill me like he did my grandmother."

The sheriff rolled his eyes. "And I thought my wife was the most stubborn woman in Misty Hollow. Don't do anything alone. Make sure Dane is with you at all times." He gave a curt nod and strode to the fire chief who was conversing with one of the firemen.

She'd comply with his orders. Tatym had no desire to be alone and taken unawares. Hurrying up to Dane and his grandmother, she asked, "Are you okay?"

"Just fine, thank you. No lasting damage. Now, let me find someone to clean the house while you take me to breakfast." She'd removed the oxygen mask. "Good thing I'm a light sleeper."

Not light enough to catch the arsonist, though. Tatym smiled.

"Alisa does my regular cleaning, but I'm guessing I need a specialist. Find me one on your phone, Dane."

"Since you're as bossy as ever, I reckon you feel just fine." He pulled his phone from his pocket. A few minutes later, he'd scheduled a team from Langley to arrive within the hour.

"It's the tail end of the breakfast rush," Tatym said. "A good time to go."

"As long as they aren't out of chocolate gravy." June held out her hand for Dane to help her to the ground.

He lifted her as if she weighed no more than a child.

"I see where Dane inherited his eating habits." Tatym grinned. "They always have plenty of gravy."

Sheriff Westbrook joined them again. "One of the firemen found this." He handed Dane a plastic envelope containing a piece of paper.

Tatym leaned over Dane's shoulder and read it

aloud. "Give me what I want, or next time someone dies."

~

Look at the fear on Dane's and Tatym's faces. He choked back a laugh while doing his best to look as horrified as the other people around him.

Now that he'd threatened the old woman, they'd know how serious he was. Even Alice Billings would've caved in over this. He should have thought of threatening her friends while she was still alive. Maybe then he wouldn't have had to resort to murder.

But, now that he had killed, he would do so again if the situation called for it.

"Bad stuff happening, huh?" Wilbur, a regular at the diner, sidled close. "This town gets a reprieve once in a while, then evil rears its evil head again. A real pity."

He couldn't keep the scowl from forming. He wasn't evil. It was his right to take what belonged to him.

"I heard Tatym found the original deed, and it still says the land belongs to her."

"Really? Where did she find it?"

Wilbur shrugged. "Somewhere up at the cabin, I reckon. Didn't say. Guess that puts that matter to rest."

Did it? Had all he'd done been for nothing? He had to take a look at that deed, but how? It would require being very careful. Becky might have turned into a nagging shrew lately, but if she found out he was the one threatening women, she'd disown him. His identity had to be kept secret until he had the money to erase all her worries.

He glanced around, studying every face to see whether anyone looked at him with suspicion.

"Are you all right, man? You seem a bit skittish."

"Worried about what's going on, that's all."

"Ain't that a fact?" Wilbur seemed a little too nosy. He sure hoped he wouldn't have to kill his friend. That might break his heart.

With a heavy sigh, he pulled a syringe from his pocket, one he thought he might have to use on June. Instead, he plunged the needle into Wilbur's arm, then slapped the spot. "Mosquito."

~

Why his grandmother? She had nothing to do with the deed or Tatym. Nothing more than having been Alice's friend. Now, Dane sat across from her and Tatym at the diner not having a clue what to do. How could he keep them both safe with one on top of the mountain and the other down in town?

Lucy bustled toward them. "You okay, June?"

"I'm fine. Someone is trying to scare me, I guess."

"Not you. Me." Tatym's voice barely rose above a whisper. "Do you have a moment, Lucy? Dane and I would like to ask you some questions."

"Sure, I do." Her forehead creased as she slid next to him.

Dane, relieved the diner was pretty empty at that hour—most folks had already dined and gone—shifted slightly in order to see her. They definitely didn't need anyone eavesdropping on their conversation. "I don't know whether you've heard, but Sheriff Westbrook has deputized me. Because of that, I have a list of potential suspects. People who use insulin or have a family member who uses it. Alice was killed by a lethal injection of insulin. Do you mind looking at the list?"

"Let me order breakfast first," Grandma said. "Researching potential murderers isn't something a person should do on an empty stomach."

They ordered breakfast. With no one in the mood for idle chitchat, they sat silent, lost in their own thoughts until their food arrived.

"All right. I can eat and read the list at the same time. Tatym, why don't you sit next to Dane and let Lucy sit next to me? That way, we don't strain our necks." Grandma cut into a biscuit slathered with chocolate gravy.

Tatym pushed her plate across the table and switched places with Lucy.

Good. Dane liked her close to him. He pulled the list from his pocket and slid it across to the other two women. "We'd like to know who on this list had a grudge against Alice or was overly interested in the alleged deed."

"No one had anything against Alice," Lucy said, reading the list of names. "The deed now, that's a whole other story. Right, June?"

"Definitely, but I don't know who would kill for the thing. I don't know anyone who actually believes the story."

"Somebody does." Dane frowned. "Tatym's being terrorized, and you were threatened. This is the whole reason we're making that fake deed." He sure wished the original hundred-year-old deed was available. But, it had vanished and a new one was made years ago. What if Tatym's copy really wasn't authentic? He voiced the thought out loud.

Tatym pulled away from him. "Are you accusing my family of stealing?"

"Not you or your grandmother, but what if?"

"That's ridiculous." She crossed her arms. "Of

course, the land belongs to my family. We've lived there a long time. Take a look at the photos on the mantel sometime. You'll see my great grandparents on that very porch. On the wall in the bedroom is a faded photo of their parents on the same porch."

"I didn't mean to offend you." He reached for her hand, only to have her snatch it back.

"This whole thing is because someone thinks about the property the same way you do." He messed up royally. Rather than say something else wrong, he dug into his biscuits and gravy.

"There are several possibilities on here." Lucy tapped the paper. "If the two of you are done arguing, I'll tell you."

"We're done," Tatym said with a huff.

"Frank Grayson has a son with diabetes; so does Kelly Turner, but since you believe the suspect to be male, that rules her out. Joe Williams has diabetes, and so does Ted Johnson's wife. I'd say the three males are your best bets. I've heard them mention the deed a time or two while dining here but didn't put too much stock into what they said. June?"

"I agree. One of those men is the one you're looking for."

The trouble was discovering which one before someone was seriously hurt, or worse. Dane could easily find a reason to pay Grayson a visit. He'd need materials to rebuild the garage. The other two men he'd never met. Extracting information from them would be trickier.

"What now?" Tatym asked without looking at him.

"We give these names to the sheriff and figure out who killed Alice." Dane glanced out the window. "Isn't that Wilbur's truck barreling toward the diner?"

Lucy's eyes widened. "I don't think he's going to stop."

"Out of the booth, now!" He shoved Tatym and slid after her before grabbing her around the waist and diving to one side.

One moment later the truck crashed through the window.

Chapter Fifteen

Tatym lay there on the floor gaping like a fish out of water as Dane said something. His lips moved, but she couldn't hear him. He ran his hands up and down her body, then scrambled across the floor to the other two women.

Cries for help rose around her as her hearing returned. With a groan, she pushed to a sitting position and stared into the pale face of Wilbur. Blood poured from a gash in the old man's forehead.

Fear spurred her to stand. She pressed two fingers to his neck. Alive.

She glanced around for her phone which had been on the table. Someone needed to call for an ambulance. Approaching sirens alerted her to the fact someone already had. "Are they all right?" She moved to Dane. "You're bleeding." A large shard of glass protruded from his shoulder.

"I'll be all right. Oher than some cuts, the ladies are okay."

"Speak for yourself." June put a hand to her head. "I collided with the booth on my way down."

Lucy and June would be fine. Other than scratches from flying pieces of glass, Tatym seemed okay. Others weren't. "I'm going to see who I can help."

"I'll come with you."

"No, your grandmother needs you, and you need medical attention. Chef Rawlings is already making the rounds. I'll help him." She silently implored him to stay still. Every time he moved, he bled harder.

He gave her a grim nod and sat hunched over on the floor next to June.

By now, several onlookers skirted the fallen bricks and shattered windows to offer what aid they could. Tatym knelt next to Heather. The girl was unconscious but alive, pinned down by one of the booths.

Tatym struggled to free her, but she didn't have the physical strength.

"Let me help." Frank Grayson slid his hands under the edge of the booth and heaved. "Pull her out."

She grasped under Heather's arms and pulled. One leg stuck out at a weird angle, a bit of bone protruding through her skin. Tatym glanced up to see the sheriff striding toward Wilbur's truck.

By now, the old man was coming to, his eyelids fluttering. When he realized he sat in his truck inside the diner, his eyes popped wide. "What in tarnation?"

"That's my question," Sheriff Westbrook asked. "You been drinking, Wilbur?"

"Nothing but water and coffee, I swear." He tried to push his door open. It didn't budge. "I'm stuck."

"Sit tight. We'll get to you in a bit." The sheriff turned to Tatym. "You okay?"

She nodded. "There are others who aren't, though." She motioned her head toward Dane, June, and Lucy. "Heather has a broken leg. That's as much as I know."

"The paramedics will be taking the worst cases first.

I'm pretty sure that includes at least Dane and Heather." He clapped a hand on her shoulder. "You're doing a good job."

She left him to his business and got back to hers.

"This guy is dead." Chef Rawlings said from a few feet away, his bald head covered with sweat.

Tatym peered into the face of a middle-aged man she didn't know. Someone who most likely had come to town to have a bite before returning home, to work, or maybe one of the vacation cabins near the lake. Now, he lay crumbled like a wadded-up napkin in the corner of the diner.

Tears sprang to her eyes. One death was one too many.

"What happened?" The chef turned a weary face her way.

"Seems Wilbur blacked out and drove through the window."

"He must have been going pretty fast to cause this much damage."

Come to think of it, he had been speeding toward them. Why? No one can enter the parking lot head-on to the diner. A median of flowers split the entrance and the exit.

Tatym moved to where the window used to be. The old man would've had to pop over the median. She moved to his car window. "Wilbur, why didn't you drive around the median?"

"I wasn't headed here. I was leaving the bakery across the street."

Which was in direct line of the diner. "Have you been feeling ill?"

"Not really, although I do have a bang-up headache

at the moment."

She could imagine. The poor thing had to have blacked out while leaving the bakery and simply floored the gas pedal.

Once the paramedics and fire department had moved everyone outside the diner, cleanup started. Lucy's wouldn't be open for a while. That left Tatym without a job, but it did give her time to discover who her intruder was.

"Tatym?" Mr. Grayson handed her the slightly ragged list of suspects and her phone. "I think these might be yours."

"Thank you." The front of her phone had been smashed. She slipped both items into her pocket and went to find Dane.

~

What was that list for? His hands curled into fists. Becky and the boys. Other women and children. His name.

He tossed bricks into the back of a pickup truck. What did they all have in common?

"Hey, dude, you're going to throw one through my window if you keep it up." The truck driver scowled over the bed of the truck.

"Sorry." He was tired of helping anyway, and it was getting close to suppertime. Becky would be pleased that he'd stayed and helped as long as he had. He waved a hand of farewell toward the sheriff and headed home.

How much did Tatym know? By the time Becky opened the door to the house to see why he hadn't entered yet, he still didn't know. With a sigh, he shoved open his door and entered the house.

"I heard about the diner." Becky cupped his cheek.

"That's awful. How bad?"

"Pretty bad. One dead, lots injured. I'm going to take a shower before we eat."

"All right, sweetheart. I'll make sure the boys stay quiet for a bit."

Under the spray of the water, he leaned against the wall, realizing for the first time he might not accomplish his goal of grabbing that land. Once he did have it, then what? Had he managed to save enough to start building his resort? He didn't think so. What he needed to do was convince Tatym to sign over the deed willingly. At least sell it to him. He could figure it out once the land was his.

But could he do that without anyone finding out the lengths he'd gone to? The choice was two-fold. Force Tatym to sell or eliminate her.

~

The glass in his shoulder hurt like Hades. Dane tried moving his left arm and groaned. The bandage made it impossible.

"That has to stay on for a few days, or you'll pull out the stitches," the doctor said. "We're seeing a lot of you lately, Mr. James."

"Wrong place at the wrong time, I guess." He smiled as a Tatym, her clothes covered in dust and her hair in disarray, rushed to the bedside. "You've been working."

"I'm exhausted." She kissed his cheek. "Sorry it took me so long to get here. Where's your shirt?"

"They cut it off me."

"From what I heard, young lady," the doctor said, "you were an amazing help to the first responders."

Her face warmed. "It's what anyone would do."

"Not everyone. I'll sign the release papers for you,

Mr. James. Try to stay out of my ER." He grinned and left them alone.

Dane sat up and used his good arm to pull Tatym close. "You're amazing." Just as he started to kiss her, the sheriff cleared his throat.

"Sorry to interrupt, but I thought you might like to know that Wilbur was on drugs when he smashed through the diner window."

"Really?" Tatym's eyes widened. "He doesn't seem the type."

The sheriff gave a wry chuckle. "Pretty sure he was drugged by someone else. He'd been at June's watching the fire, then went to pick up some doughnuts. That's the last thing the poor man remembers. Can't remember who all he spoke to at the fire either."

Dane frowned. "Slow-acting drug."

"Since we don't know who gave it to him, we have no way of knowing how fast or slow. Be careful heading home. There's a storm coming."

"Looks like I'll be doing the driving for a while." Tatym sat in the chair across from him. "Does it hurt much?"

"Yep, but I'll live, and there's no lasting damage." He turned her face to his. "A kiss—"

"Here you go, sir." A nurse handed him several papers. "You're free to go."

Tatym stood and held out her hand. "I'll kiss you in the car."

"Then why aren't we running?" He grinned.

"Because you won't be doing that for a few days." Her cheeks warmed again. "I'm also out of a job, so we'll be on the mountain a lot. How is June?"

He took her hand and headed for the parking lot.

"Taken straight home from the diner. Lucy will be staying with her for a few days, and a squad car will drive by several times a day and night."

Tatym took a deep breath. "If you'd feel better staying here…"

"Not without you."

Her shoulders sagged. "Then, we'll pick up Ebony and come back to town."

"Really?" She'd make that sacrifice for him? "It would make me feel better." To have the two women he cared about under the same roof. It would be nice not to have his heart torn between the two of them…which one needed him the most.

"It's only until this threat is gone."

He leaned close to whisper, "I'll make sure my grandmother plays nice."

She giggled. "She's not that bad. Just opinionated and outspoken and blunt."

"That she is." After opening the driver's side door for her, he struggled to the passenger side. There'd be no pace faster than a slug. Every movement jostled his shoulder and pulled at the stitches. He glanced at the sky overhead. No moonlight or stars pierced the thick clouds. Humidity hung in the air. They'd be lucky to make it back before the storm.

"Do you think there will be tornados?" Tatym started the truck.

"I'll look at the radar on my phone." Dane shifted and pulled his phone from his pocket. "Heavy rain, strong winds, and hail. No tornados predicted." Still, he didn't like the heaviness in the air.

"You look worried." Tatym headed for the mountain.

"It'll be fine. We can't leave Ebony up there by herself with thunderstorms coming. Dogs don't like storms. Let's not dawdle."

"Don't plan on it." She increased their speed.

The heavens opened half a mile from her cabin. Rain they could handle. He shoved open his door and made his way to the house.

By the time they stepped inside, Dane was soaked through. "Let me change while you pack a few things."

"I don't think we're leaving for a while."

Hail beat on the roof. The rain came sideways.

A mighty crack sounded outside. Dane moved to the front porch in time to see a large oak tree fall behind his truck. They were definitely stuck until someone came out to clear the road.

A flash of lightning followed closely by the roar of thunder had Tatym ducking and Ebony darting under the table. They were definitely in for a loud night.

Dane shivered and went to change as the lights went out. He couldn't see his hand in front of his face.

"I have candles," Tatym called after him. "Don't move." Something fell as Tatym felt her way around the room. A few minutes later, she handed him a tapered candle in a holder. "There's an oil lamp, too. I'll light that, then go change myself."

Dane quickly changed into dry pants and slung a towel around his shoulders when the sleeve wouldn't fit over his wounded arm. It might be summer, but the storm brought cooler temperatures.

From the other room, Ebony started to bark. A slow woof at first, then frenzied yaps. Something slammed against the front door.

Chapter Sixteen

Dane rushed from the room, ignoring the agonizing pain in his shoulder that each footfall caused. "Don't open that door."

Tatym froze in the middle of the living room. "I wasn't planning on it, but I do want to look outside. Hush, Ebony."

The dog's barks turned to a whimper.

It could be nothing more than something blown onto the porch, but Dane wasn't taking any chances. He returned to his room for his gun, then peered out the peephole. Not seeing anything, he inched open the curtain. With the rain and wind so fierce, he couldn't see past the porch or in front of the door. He'd have to open it. "Stay back." He turned the deadlock and opened the door. A tree branch lay on the porch. "Just the storm." He closed and relocked the door. "It's going to be a long night."

"I'll make coffee." Tatym headed to the kitchen counter. "Oh. Can't without power. Isn't it strange how one thing can interfere with habits?"

Dane gave her a worried look. Why was she concerned about coffee at a time like this?

The dog now scratched at the back door. Maybe it

wasn't only a tree branch. Something, or someone, prowled the yard. With the electricity out, the cameras were useless, and Dane really didn't want to go out there.

"What is it?" Tatym turned from the coffeepot.

"I don't know. Something's out there. Ebony acts as if it's not the storm." Dane pulled out a chair and sat at the table. "I'll take a look when the wind and rain die down."

"You should rest. You look terrible."

"Thanks." He chuckled. "I won't be able to rest with this storm."

She set a cup of coffee in front of him. "Anything I can do to ease your pain? Bring you a pill?"

"No, thanks." He wanted to be coherent in case it wasn't the storm bothering the dog. Pain meds made him fuzzy.

The wind continued to batter the house for the next hour before slowly easing, then the rain stopped. Dane stood and went to stand on the porch while Ebony relieved herself in the yard.

The dog stopped, her hackles raised. She growled, then bared her teeth.

Dane followed the dog's stare. A man in a yellow raincoat, the type big sea fishermen wore, stood where the road down the mountain began, the yellow of his coat bright against the fallen tree.

"Do you know who it is?" Tatym stood close enough to him he could feel her body heat.

"I'm guessing it's our mysterious intruder." Everything in him wanted to give chase, but having his arm in a sling made him usher Tatym and Ebony inside. "Double-check that the windows are locked."

"You think he'll do more than scare us?" She paled.

"Eventually. Maybe tonight, maybe not, but we should always assume he's going to." Dane locked the front door and checked the back.

A few minutes later, footsteps paced on the porch. Something scraped along the wall, sending Ebony into a frenzy.

Tatym gripped her gun like a lifeline. Dane had his within easy reach.

Scare tactics. The man simply wanted to intimidate, but he was doing a good job.

Adrenaline burned through Dane's veins. Perspiration trickled down his bare back.

"I almost wish he'd make a move," Tatym whispered. "This is driving me crazy."

Dane turned in a circle as the scraping went around the house.

The window in the back door shattered.

Tatym screamed.

Dane stared at a rock the size of his fist. Paper had been tied around it with a piece of twine. "Fetch, Ebony." He stayed between Tatym and the door.

The dog retrieved the rock and dropped it into Dane's outstretched hand. He then handed it to Tatym to untie.

"*Are you ready to sell now*?" She read. "Is he crazy? If I did put this place up for sale, we'd know the person who bought it was the one who threw this."

"The longer this goes on, the more unhinged he becomes."

"Well, I won't sell. Do you hear me?" She shouted. "I will never sell this place."

"Then you will meet the same fate as your grandmother," the man growled.

"So be it." Tatym shot Dane a sharp look. "You with me?"

He quirked his mouth. "Can't let you have all the fun, can I?"

The lights flickered on.

Tatym grabbed her phone and pulled up the app for the cameras in time for them to see the man sprint toward the road.

~

He sped dangerously fast down the wet mountain road. How dare Tatym defy him? He didn't want to kill again. Why couldn't people be reasoned with?

He gripped the steering wheel as his truck careened around a corner, then fishtailed. If he had a wreck because that woman made his blood boil, he'd kill Dane and anyone else she might care for.

Becky was waiting for him at home, her face mottled with red. "What is so important you had to go out late in a storm like this?"

"I was already out. Can't help it if a storm came up. I stayed at the office until it stopped." He was becoming tired of her harping. "Please don't nag. It's been a long night."

"Is your phone broken?" She crossed her arms. "You could've called me."

"No electricity, and I don't know where my cell phone is." He patted his pockets. Where was the darn thing? "Could you call it? Maybe it fell between the seat and the console." He opened the door to his truck and casually knocked the phone off the seat.

"All right." She returned to the house.

Seconds later, his phone rang. "Got it."

"I'm sorry I was angry," she said. "It's just that I

worry when you're out in bad weather." She cupped his cheek. "Forgive me?"

"Of course." He grinned. Again, all was perfect in his world. Almost. Now, to take care of what kept it from being perfect. He'd lay low for a few days to pacify Becky and give Tatym a chance to let her guard down, then he'd strike the final blow.

~

"Do you know how many men in town have a raincoat like that?" Sheriff Westbrook's brow furrowed as he spoke over the sound of chainsaws cutting the fallen tree.

"Can you see how many of our insulin suspects have one?" Tatym cocked her head. "We can't keep doing this. He gave me a direct threat last night, admitting he killed my grandmother."

"Not exactly. You told me he said you'd suffer the same fate. That most likely wouldn't hold up in a court of law." He glanced at Dane. "You okay?"

"Been better. As soon as the road is clear, I'm moving Tatym to my grandmother's house."

"Good. We already have a squad car doing regular patrols. It'll be safer. See you in town." He turned and marched away.

"He sure didn't seem overly concerned about our visitor last night." She frowned.

"Nothing he can do until we find out who we're looking for. I'm going to gather up the few things I have here. They'll have the road unblocked soon."

She needed to pack, too. Pausing in the doorway, she glanced around at what had quickly become her favorite place to be. How long until she could watch the sun lift the mist again? What if that man came back and burned down her home?

If he did, she'd rebuild as many times as she needed to. The man hadn't met stubborn until meeting her. She took after her grandmother, after all.

By midday the road had been cleared. They left her truck behind, Dane promising they'd return for hers when he could drive.

"Will your grandmother care about Ebony?" Some people weren't keen on dogs in the house.

"She'll have to be. We can't stay here, and we can't leave the dog on her own." He opened the door and motioned for Ebony to jump inside before sliding in himself.

Tatym slid into the driver's seat. "I really hope I can come back here soon." Tears stung her eyes.

"You will, sweetheart. I'll do everything in my power to make it happen."

She nodded and turned the key in the ignition. At least he hadn't promised.

When they arrived, June's brows lowered at the sight of Ebony. "I hope she's housebroken."

"She is." Tatym smiled. "She can stay in the sunroom if you prefer."

"Let's see how badly she sheds." She stepped aside so they could enter. "Had to hear through the grapevine again that my grandson was injured."

"I'm sorry. There's been a lot going on." Dane went to kiss her cheek only to have her turn her head. "Grandma."

Tatym raised her brows and set her suitcase on the floor. "Which room is mine?"

"Second floor, third door on the right. Dane is the first door. A Jack-n-Jill bathroom separates the two rooms. Do I have to worry about hanky-panky?"

"No, ma'am." Tatym's face heated. She couldn't reach the stairs fast enough.

Her temporary home held a four-poster bed covered with a vintage white bedspread. An armoire stood in the corner. Gauzy white curtains adorned the window. She couldn't see the street from her room but had a nice view of the backyard. A few tree limbs lay scattered around the yard. She'd clean them up when she finished unpacking.

Ebony whined, her tail thumping on the floor.

"Sorry, girl. You'll have a fenced-in yard for a bit. It's only temporary." She could only pray it was so.

When she returned downstairs, Dane and June sat at the kitchen table, coffee and cookies in front of them. "I'll be outside with Ebony, cleaning up branches blown down last night."

"That's my job," Dane said.

"You can't do much with one arm. You're supposed to be resting. Don't you want full use of that arm again?" She shook her head and headed outside. Once the yard was clean, she'd head to the diner to see if she could help there. Idleness would drive her nuts.

What would June think if she knew Dane had kissed Tatym? What about the kiss? What exactly was Tatym to Dane? Were they in a relationship or simply deriving comfort from each other during a rough time? The biggest question was what did she want? She hadn't planned on a relationship so soon after arriving in Misty Hollow. Tatym gave a sarcastic chuckle. Hadn't planned on someone wanting to harm her or her grandmother's death being a murder either.

Soon, she'd gathered a small pile of branches and

set them on fire. Smoke rose into a clear blue sky, so pretty after such a violent storm.

Dane watched from the back deck. "You look miles away."

"Trying to figure everything out. In a bit, I'm heading to the diner to help with cleanup and repairs."

"Wish I could be of more use."

"You won't be in a sling for long." She smiled. "It'll do you good to spend time with June. For a person who doesn't like to leave her house, this must all be weighing on her."

"It is." He sat in an Adirondack chair and stretched out his legs. "I'm not going to enjoy these few days of leisure."

"Try. Things are going to heat up very quickly."

Chapter Seventeen

Tatym stopped in the bustling parking lot of Lucy's Diner. The aroma of cooking food drifted through the air. Picnic tables had been set up at one end of the lot and were full of people. Business went on, it seemed.

Smiling, she went to don her apron. "Glad to see you didn't shut down."

"Glad to see you showed up for work." Lucy brushed the back of her hand across her perspiring brow. "It's hot, but folks still came. If it doesn't rain before the diner is fixed, we'll keep on outside. Table six needs their order delivered."

"Got it." She hurried to the serving window. Table six hosted the Grayson family. "Good afternoon."

"Same to you, Tatym." Frank sniffed his burger. "My men will have the front wall fixed within a few days, and we appreciate y'all serving us."

"Our pleasure." She moved to the next table and took their order. By the time Dane and June showed up to check on why she was still there, perspiration ran down her back.

"You're working." He smiled, ushering June to a table. "Guess we'll have supper here."

"You are supposed to be resting." She arched a brow.

"That's what I said, but the man is as stubborn as a mule." June sat. "He lay down for maybe fifteen minutes."

"It was over an hour, and you know it." Dane shook his head. "I'm surprised to see Tatym working after a sleepless night."

"I'll go to bed early." She was tired. More tired than she could remember being, but she had a job to do, one where she was needed. As grandma used to say, she could catch up on her sleep when she was dead. Tatym cleared the table vacated by the Graysons, took the dishes to the kitchen, and collapsed in a chair for a two-minute break. "The other gal couldn't make it?"

"She'll be in tomorrow," Lucy said. "Made plans not thinking we'd be open."

"I came to help with the cleanup." Tatym laughed. "I had no idea you'd be open for business."

"Gotta pay the bills." She laughed and carried an order to a table.

"Here." Chef Rawlings thrust a cup of coffee into her hand. "It's cooled enough to drink."

"You're an angel." She breathed the aroma and took a sip. The coffee would help her make it through the last hour of her shift.

"You're having quite the time of it, aren't you? Up at the cabin?"

Tatym narrowed her eyes. "How'd you know that?"

"Folks are talking." He shrugged. "People are saying you found the deed that's been rumored about for years."

"I suppose I have." She took another sip of her

coffee while she tried to figure out where the conversation was headed.

"I wouldn't carry it on your person."

"Too smart for that." Spiders skittered down her spine, mixing with the sweat that now ran cold.

"Good." He grinned. "I knew you had a good head on your shoulders." The chef returned to the stove.

In the time she'd been working at the diner, she'd never had such a lengthy conversation with the chef. She studied his form. He seemed a bit large to move as fast as the man who kept coming around did, but should she add him to the suspect list?

She sighed and pushed to her feet, ready to finish the evening and go to bed. The parking lot was now lit up with large lights to enable the construction workers to continue working. She wished them luck.

A man in pressed trousers and a tie stood at Dane's table. He handed Dane a large manila envelope. Dane handed him cash.

Tatym's heart leaped to her throat. Could it be the deed? She glanced back at the chef who seemed oblivious, focused on the stove. Several others watched the transaction between Dane and the stranger but soon returned to what they were doing.

Dane glanced up and smiled. The gesture set her heart at rest. Everything would turn out fine. She could feel it deep within her.

She peered at the crowd around them, mainly men at this point. Knowing things would be fine didn't mean the danger was over. Being fine didn't mean she'd make it out of this alive. It just meant things would be as they were meant to be. The thought somehow brought a bit of comfort.

Off to the side, she caught Frank Grayson intently watching the exchange between Dane and the other man. When he saw her watching him, he turned and strode to his truck.

People were acting very strange this evening. It could be because of the accident or the severe storm the night before. Either way, Tatym's nerves twanged so much she felt a headache coming on.

"Go on home." Lucy patted her shoulder. "You've done enough today. See you at ten in the morning and not a minute before. I can finish up here."

"Are you sure?"

"Absolutely."

Tatym didn't need to be told twice. She joined Dane and June. "I'm off."

"Wonderful." He slid the envelope across the table. "It's here. Time for phase two of Operation Deed. Let's hope our guy saw the exchange."

~

"We're getting close." She picked up the envelope and cradled it to her chest. "What is the next step?"

Sheriff Westbrook and one of the builders approached their table. "Lemley has something you might want to hear."

Dane nodded. "Go ahead."

"Well, you remember that night of the accident? Not Wilbur's, but the one up the mountain?"

"When the deer was hit?"

"Yeah. Anyway, the sheriff here has been asking a lot of questions, and this seems a bit suspicious to me."

Dane wanted to tell the man to spit it out. "Okay…"

"Well, Frank Grayson was headed down the mountain when we hit that deer. He stopped and turned his truck around when he reached us. That was right before you arrived."

"I was working up at Tatym's place that day. I didn't see Frank." So far, nothing seemed overly suspicious. "Y'all were delivering an order. Frank could've have gone to check to see whether I had arrived." He glanced at the sheriff. "Am I missing something?"

"Frank Grayson wasn't supposed to be up there. He told his men he had a job out of town."

"That's right," Lemley said, bobbing his head like one of the toy dogs people had on their dashboards. "Imagine our surprise to see him." He lowered his voice and leaned closer. "He's been real interested in that rumor, too. The one about the deed. Talks about it all the time."

And one of his sons used insulin. Dane glanced across the lot to where Grayson watched them, a stony look on his face. Then, he got into his truck and drove away. Was the angry look because he was the man they were looking for or because his worker was talking instead of working?

"Thanks, Lemley. You can go." The sheriff pulled up a seat. "At this time, Grayson is our main suspect. I want the two of you to be very careful, especially after the man showed up at Tatym's place during that bad storm."

"I heard tell," Grandma said, "that his wife, Becky, has been complaining that he's gone way into the night, sometimes not coming home until morning. I thought maybe he had a mistress, but now I bet it's because he's up there harassing Tatym."

The sheriff's face grew grave. "That makes a lot of sense to me. I'll send a deputy over to speak to his wife and bring Frank in for questioning." He glanced at the envelope. "The fake deed?"

"Yes." Tatym nodded. "I'm not sure it's needed anymore."

He stood. "You might need it to trade if Frank gets his hands on you."

"That sounds like a warning."

"It is. The more I know about what he's been doing, the more concerned I am." He gave a sharp nod and strode away.

"Can we go home now?" Tatym asked. "I'm going to fall asleep right here."

"Yes, of course. I'm sorry." He struggled to his feet and helped his grandmother to hers. "We could all use a good night's sleep." If he could sleep at all after the sheriff's words. He had a feeling he'd be keeping watch most of the night. If Frank was their guy and he suspected they knew, he'd make his move.

Back at the house, Tatym headed straight to bed, followed shortly by his grandmother, leaving it up to Dane to take the dog out. He didn't mind. It gave him a chance to do a perimeter check before he turned in.

Locking the door so no one could sneak in behind him, he flicked on a flashlight and walked slowly along the chain-link fence that enclosed the yard. He didn't expect to see anything out of the ordinary but wanted to get a lay of the land so when he checked again in the morning, he'd know whether they had a visitor.

Ebony didn't seem bothered. Instead, nose to the ground, she explored the yard, occasionally glancing up at Dane. By the time they completed walking the perimeter, exhaustion weighed on Dane's shoulders.

He wouldn't be able to stay awake. Best thing he

could do was make a bed on the sofa. Anyone coming in the house would have to go past him to go upstairs. "Come on, girl." Dane slapped his thigh. "You're sleeping downstairs with me tonight. I need your ears." Inside, he checked all the doors and windows before stretching out on the flowered sofa that had seen better days. At least the throw pillow was soft.

The sun streaming through a crack in the curtains and the smell of frying bacon woke him the next morning. He leaped to his feet as if an alarm had gone off.

"Why'd you let me sleep so long?" He asked his grandmother in the kitchen.

"Because you needed the sleep. Tatym hasn't woke yet, but I did peek in on her. She's fine. Sit. Breakfast is ready."

"Thanks." He dug into the scrambled eggs, bacon, and toast as if he hadn't eaten in days. As he ate, he tried to figure out their next move. Should they wait for Frank to make the move? Stay tight until the sheriff said they had him in custody? Was Frank even the culprit?

"I can hear the wheels in your head spinning. Want to talk about it?"

"Not sure what to say at this point."

"I want to talk to Becky Grayson." Tatym entered the kitchen. "If we lay everything out in front of her, she'll know whether her husband is the one we want."

"She might not talk."

Tatym gave a one-shoulder shrug. "She might not, but she also might, and I'm willing to try. I don't have time before work, but we can pay her a visit right after. If we see Frank's truck, we'll wait for another time."

"I know her," Grandma said. "Dane and I will talk

to her after dropping you off at work. Frank will be working by then."

"What has happened to you?" Dane smiled. "You've gone from never leaving the house to turning detective."

"Life is too short. Plus, I'm enjoying the adventure. Keeps the heart pumping."

Dane shot an amused glance at Tatym. It wasn't the adventure that sped up his heart.

~

Frank stopped his truck on a dirt road a few miles out of town and drummed his fingers on the steering wheel. Did they know? Was the original deed in that envelope that the young man handed Dane? Fury burned through him. A snip of a girl had ruined his life, thwarted his plans, taken away his dreams. The land would never belong to him. He'd never be rich and ease his wife's burden of raising a son with diabetes. Tatym needed to pay for what she'd taken from him.

How, though? If they did suspect him, they'd be looking for him. He couldn't go home. He couldn't work. He'd have to hide. But where?

The sheriff would go to his house and speak with Becky. She'd tell him all about Frank's late nights. He had no way to warn her and tell her everything would be fine.

He was up against a wall with no way out. All he could do was exact revenge for what he'd lost.

Chapter Eighteen

Tatym hadn't been happy at all that he and his grandmother had gone to question Becky Grayson without her. It couldn't be helped. They were running out of time. Frank could be moving away.

"Step aside. She knows me." Grandma pushed her way to the front. "You just follow my lead."

"As you wish." He grinned and gave her a mock bow as she pressed the doorbell.

"Don't be insolent." Her mouth twitched. "Let's get justice for my friend."

A pretty woman around the age of forty opened the door, a questioning look on her face. "June?"

"Yep. Mind if my grandson and I come in?"

"Sure." She stepped back and held the door open. "The boys are playing in the backyard."

"We'll make this quick. It isn't a subject they should hear." Grandma bustled forward and sat on a pleather sofa. "Have a seat, dear." She motioned for Becky to sit across from her, leaving the rest of the sofa for Dane.

"We're actually here on official sheriff business," he said. "I'm Deputy James, and I'd like to ask you some questions about your husband."

"Frank?" She clutched the neckline of her blouse.

"Is he okay?"

"Do you know where your husband is?"

She shook her head. "He didn't come home last night. What is this about?"

Dane wanted to wish away the fear in the woman's eyes, but knew he had to lay what they knew in front of her. "We believe Frank has been terrorizing Tatym Billings. He's also the primary person of interest in the death of Tatym's grandmother."

"Absolutely not." She shook her head hard enough for a few strands of hair to pull free from the bun she wore. "Frank would never harm anyone." A flicker of doubt crossed her features.

"Has he been staying out late, acting secretive?" Grandma leaned forward. "Kind of like a man having an affair?"

Becky clenched her hands in her lap. "That's what I thought he was up to. *Think* he's up to." She hitched her chin. "My husband doesn't prey on women. Why would he risk his life and our family's?"

"Has he been talking recently about a deed or coming into money?" Dane raised a brow.

"He's mentioned a few times how our future looked brighter." Tears sprang to her eyes. "You're serious?"

"Yes, ma'am. Do you have any idea where your husband might be hiding?"

She jumped to her feet and peered out the kitchen window. With a shaky exhale, she turned to face them. "I have no idea. Other than this house and the business, we have nothing. I'm going to pack a few things and take the boys to my parents." Resignation lined her face. "Frank has been different lately. Full of anger and secrets. I thought it would pass."

"I understand one of your sons is diabetic."

She gave a wary nod.

"Has some insulin come up missing over the last few months?"

Her mouth gaped open. "Yes, how did you know? Frank told me the pharmacy shorted us."

"I'm sorry, Mrs. Grayson." Dane pushed to his feet and handed her a business card. "If you hear from your husband, please contact the sheriff's office."

"Let us know if you need anything." Grandma rushed forward and wrapped the woman in a hug. "I'll add you to the church's prayer chain."

"Thank you, but don't tell them why. If you'll see yourself out, I'll fetch my boys." Becky's shoulders slumped as she headed out the back door.

Outside, Grandma linked her arm with Dane's. "Now that we've ruined that poor woman's day, what's next?"

"We need to find out where Frank is hiding. I'd like to visit his construction office."

"I'm sure it's past hours."

He chuckled. "All the better. Ready for some snooping?" It probably wasn't a good idea to take her along, but he wasn't going to leave her behind. Not with Frank on the loose.

A bright motion light flickered to life as they pulled in front of a large metal building sitting on several acres of concrete piled with building supplies. Trucks and construction material filled the lot. A dog barked somewhere in the distance. Before they could get out of the car, a man exited the building and marched toward them.

"Hey, Dane. What brings you out here this late?"

Roy Jones, a man Dane had run across a few times in town, leaned his arms on the truck door.

"Looking for Frank."

"Ain't seen him since he left the diner yesterday."

"Any idea where he might hole up?"

"Home?"

Dane shook his head. "His wife hasn't seen him."

The man's brow furrowed. "He in trouble?"

"We're just looking for him."

"Since you're recently deputized, it's a mite suspicious that you'd show up here at this time of the night looking for him." As he noticed Grandma, he smiled. "Good evening, ma'am."

"Hello. Please tell Frank that Dane is looking for him if he should show up. It's nothing serious." She gave a smile that only Dane knew was anything but sweet. "Tell him Becky is worried. That's all."

He slapped the door frame. "That I can do if he comes around. See ya." He turned and headed back to the building.

"This was a waste of time," she said.

"Not really. At least we know he hasn't been here." Where are you hiding, Grayson?

~

Frank leaned his seat back as far as it would go, which wasn't very far in the cab of his truck. He stared at the ceiling. Another night sleeping in his truck. Sniffing his armpit, he wrinkled his nose. He needed a shower. Could he sneak into his house after the boys went to bed? Maybe a truck stop would be best. The sooner the better before the sheriff put out an APB, if he hadn't already.

He returned his seat to an upright position. After a

shower, he'd park between two big rigs and sleep. No one would expect him to be in the open like that. After a good night's sleep, one where he didn't jerk awake at every snap of a twig outside, he could plan his next move.

Twenty minutes later, after purchasing a new tee shirt and a baseball cap from the truck-stop store, he stood under the spray of hot water. Heaven was the only word that came to mind. Strange how something as simple as a shower could make a man feel like…a man again.

He dried off with paper towels the best he could and donned an Arkansas Razorback shirt and cap, then oversized sunglasses, which made him pretty much unrecognizable. Back in the store, he purchased two hot dogs and a coke. He had to be careful or the cash he had on hand would run out faster than he wanted.

Slipping into his house unnoticed needed to be his top priority. He had money stashed in a few places Becky didn't know about.

Back in his truck, he ate the hot dogs. Tomorrow was the day Becky visited her friend and the boys played with the woman's children. The house would be empty around nine o'clock. If he slipped in through the back, all the trees and shrubs he'd hated planting would provide him with much needed protection.

He grinned—he could do this.

~

Tatym had gone to sleep disappointed after hearing Becky Grayson had no idea where her husband was or what he'd been doing. The next morning, she sat on her bed and stared out the window at June's garage. This being her day off would give her some time to sift through the burned ruins of her own garage. There might be a few things she could salvage before Dane started to rebuild. She brought up the subject at breakfast. "June can sit on the front porch and enjoy the view."

"Sounds like a plan to me," June said. "You do own a lovely piece of property."

"Okay. I'd like to start the cleanup and order supplies. It's only a matter of time before Grayson Construction is shut down." Dane piled his plate with eggs and bacon. "Which means I'll have to order from a place in Langley. Might take a day or two longer."

"There's no rush." Tatym nibbled on a piece of toast. She marveled at how much food Dane consumed. It was a wonder the man kept so trim. Her gaze fell on his muscular arms. Maybe it took a lot of calories to keep him looking so good. She tore her gaze away, locking eyes with a very amused June. Face heating, she snatched a piece of bacon from the plate in the center of the table and focused on breakfast.

When they'd finished, they piled into Dane's truck and headed up the mountain.

Tatym held her breath until the cabin came into view. She wouldn't be surprised to find one day that Frank had also set fire to her home. So far, all he'd done was issue warnings. How much longer until he moved past warnings? Well, Dane could attest to the fact he already had, but so far he hadn't tried to harm her. Why?

She climbed from the truck after Dane and let Ebony out of the back. "Look around, girl."

While Dane helped his grandmother to a rocker on the porch, Tatym stepped to the cliff. It seemed ages since she'd watched the sun rise. Still, the sun and the mist wouldn't go anywhere. They'd be waiting when she returned home. With a sigh, she turned to the garage.

"You okay?" Dane glanced up from where he tossed aside scorched beams with his good arm.

"I'll be fine." She grabbed one end of a long two-by-four, leaving him the other end. "With you injured, maybe we should have hired someone to do the cleaning." This would be slow going.

"We can do it together." He led the way to a pile of debris. "There's no hurry, is there?"

She shook her head. To hurry would make their time together shorter. When she had no more work for him, he'd leave. Tatym never thought it possible that his leaving would fill her with sadness. But, there were the kisses. Maybe they meant something—something she could hold onto. "Look." She dug a metal box from a pile of ashes. "Grandma kept another of these in her closet. It holds important documents. What could be in this one?"

She carried it to the back patio. The fire hadn't burned through the box, so anything inside would have been preserved. Tatym took a deep breath and opened the lid. The box was stuffed with receipts. "More things for me to go through." She hadn't even started going through her grandmother's things. Her heart wasn't in it. Not with danger stalking her every move.

She lifted the top piece of paper, a printed form. "Dane, this says Grayson Construction." She unfolded the slim slip of paper. "My grandmother had hired Frank to do some repairs on the cabin. He signed this estimate the day she died." Her gaze collided with his.

"This proves he was here that day." He took the paper. "We need to take this to the sheriff. The odds against Frank keep stacking up."

"There's no doubt in my mind who's been stalking

me." She peered at the trees behind the cabin.

Her skin prickled. Was he watching them at this moment?

Chapter Nineteen

The house seemed strangely quiet. Not because Becky and the boys were at a friend's house, but as if no one lived there.

Frank's heart beat in his throat as he moved through the house. Nothing seemed out of the ordinary until he reached his oldest son's room. The closet door hung open, and drawers were partially pulled out of the dresser. He found the same in his other son's room.

Now, he ran to the master bedroom. The bed was made. Everything seemed to be in order, but Becky would never have allowed the boys to leave their rooms in such disarray. His heart stopped in the master bathroom. No sign of any of Becky's toiletries.

His toothbrush stood lonely in the holder. His wife had left, taking the boys with her.

He doubled up his fist and landed a good punch on the mirror, shattering the glass. Blood dripped from his knuckles. The loss of his family was one more strike against Tatym.

The hiding places his wife knew about were empty as he'd suspect they'd be if she'd run off. Still, there were other places he'd hidden money. Places no one knew about but him. Tucked in the walls behind light switches—a fire hazard, yes, but the house hadn't burned down, had it? He'd stuffed some cash in a frozen bag of lima beans in the freezer in the garage. Since no one liked lima beans, it had been a safe place. And finally, he felt for the envelope taped beneath his underwear drawer. Once gathered together, he had more than a thousand dollars in his hand.

His smile faded as the doorbell rang. Without moving the curtain, he peered down into the street.

The sheriff's car sat parked in the driveway. The man backed away from the porch, his gaze studying the upstairs windows. Did he know Frank hid behind the floral drapes? He reached for the gun tucked in his waistband.

The sheriff circled the house. Seconds later, footsteps sounded in the kitchen. Idiot. Frank had left the back door unlocked. He slipped into the master closet, squeezing behind some of Becky's long gowns. If the sheriff discovered his hiding spot, Frank's face would be the last one the man saw.

He listened, holding his breath, clutching his gun as the sheriff moved through his house. Intruding, looking where he shouldn't. Invading Frank's privacy.

The closet door opened, then closed, and he released a pent-up breath. A preliminary search. Frank wouldn't have to shoot the man.

~

Tatym and Dane sat on her back deck and enjoyed bowls of ice cream. They'd stopped by the sheriff's office earlier only to find him gone and left a message for him to contact them.

"I feel guilty eating ice cream so early in the day." She spooned a healthy dose of vanilla covered with chocolate syrup. "It's not even lunchtime."

"Don't tell anyone, but sometimes when there's cake, I'll have some for supper." Dane winked. "I figure as an adult, I'm free to do as I please."

"Somehow it doesn't surprise me that you would have cake for supper." What was astonishing was that *she* was eating sugar. Tatym tried to avoid it like a disease. Her empty bowl sat on the table beside her as the sound of a vehicle came from the front of the house.

"That's most likely the sheriff." Dane pushed to his feet, leaving Tatym to follow as Westbrook rounded the corner and joined them on the deck.

"Heard y'all came looking for me?" Sheriff Westbrook nodded at June.

"We have some information for you—" Tatym said, "that leaves no doubt that Frank Grayson is the man responsible. Would you like some ice cream?"

His eyes widened. "No, thanks, but I'll take a cup of coffee if you have some."

"Coffee's on." June stood. "I'll bring it out."

Dane took his seat and finished off his mid-morning treat.

"We started cleaning up the burned-down garage." Tatym pushed the contract toward the sheriff. "Found this. It proves Frank was here the day my grandmother died—"

"And," Dane interjected, "Becky Grayson confirmed there was missing insulin around that time. I'm not one to believe in coincidences."

"Neither am I. Thanks." The sheriff accepted a cup of coffee from June. "I stopped by the Grayson place this morning. No sign of anyone being there, although the back door was left unlocked.”

“Becky told us she would be taking the boys to her parents.” June stirred sugar into her cup. “They could have left in a hurry and forgot to lock the door.”

Made sense to Tatym. “We have the proof we need but no Frank.”

“My men are searching every motel, hotel, and bed and breakfast for twenty miles. He won’t have gone far. Not when he still wants something you have.”

June slapped the table. “We forgot to tell Becky we found the deed.”

“It’s not about the deed anymore.” The ice cream sat like a rock in Tatym’s stomach. “I’m the proverbial fly in Frank’s ointment. He’ll be coming for revenge. I feel it in my gut.”

“Don’t invite trouble,” June said.

“I’m not, and I haven’t. All I did was move into this cabin, my inheritance. I love this place, always have, but it’s been nothing but trouble since day one.” Tears stung the back of her eyes. “Then, finding out my grandmother was murdered topped it all off.”

“Do you regret coming here?” Worry clouded Dane’s face.

“No, I wish it was different, that’s all.” She forced a smile. “What’s next?”

“You three try to stay out of trouble while my department finds this man.” The sheriff took a swig of his coffee. “Thanks, ma’am. I’d better go to the office. Mind if I take this contract? It could be evidence.”

Tatym nodded. She had no need for it. “I’ll let you know if we find anything else.” Something she doubted. What else could possibly be left behind? If her grandmother had tried leaving a clue, Tatym would've found it by now. Not to mention the fact she'd died of an insulin overdose to mimic a heart attack. She doubted her grandmother would've seen the attack coming in time to leave Tatym anything. The deed to this place had been hers to inherit since the day she was born.

As Dane walked the sheriff to his car, her gaze fell on the thick stand of trees behind her home. Was Frank there watching? The mountain had plenty of places for a body to hide if they didn't want to be found. The only way to catch Frank was for him to come for her. "We need to set a trap," she said softly.

"Dane will never go for it." June arched a brow.

"Then we won't tell him."

~

With Frank having ghostly skills at not being seen, Dane didn't feel confident in his role of protecting Tatym and his grandmother. Nor did he feel as if he deserved the deputy badge, even if only temporary.

As if to remind him he wasn't working to his full capacity, the stitches in his shoulder pulled. All he could do was pray he didn't have a physical fight with Frank. At this point, the older man would definitely win. Dane's feet froze in place at the corner of the house as Tatym mentioned setting a trap. Then, after she said not to tell him, he stormed to the deck. "That's the dumbest thing anyone has ever said."

She hitched her chin. "Do you have a better idea? Want to sit and wait for him to shoot us sniper-style or burn the cabin down with us in it?" She tilted her head. "I'm listening."

He had nothing. "We wait. The sheriff will find Frank."

"Hasn't yet." She lunged to her feet. "I'm grabbing a few more of my things before we head back to town."

After she'd gone into the house, his grandmother spoke. "She's right. We're sitting ducks waiting for an ice storm to freeze us in the water."

"It's too dangerous. I can't protect her." His heart dropped to his knees. "Not injured as I am. We should go somewhere until this is all over."

"Never took you for someone who flees from a fight."

"Not much I can do with one arm." Not to mention the fact he'd never cared for someone the way he did Tatym. To lose her now would rip out his heart.

Grandma narrowed her eyes. "Hogwash. You'll use both arms when you have to. Chin up. Face this challenge like the man I know you are."

"I'm not a coward." His face heated.

"No, you're not. So, figure out how to save the girl." She pushed to her feet. "I'm too old for these types of adventures. Let's bring this to an end."

Easier said than done. Dane dropped to the deck stairs. Was setting a trap the only way? Wasn't that what the fake deed was supposed to do? Draw Frank out of hiding? That idea had failed miserably.

He needed to break into the construction office. Search the Grayson house. There had to be a clue somewhere as to where Frank might be. No one could disappear completely.

His cell phone vibrated. He fished it out of his pocket and read the text from the sheriff. *Grayson spotted last night at a truck stop. Meet me at the office.*

Springing to his feet, Dane rushed into the house. "Frank has been spotted. Let's go."

"When? Where?" Tatym slung a backpack over her shoulder.

"A truck stop last night. It's doubtful he's still there, but we might find out something." Hope reared its beautiful head.

The three of them rushed to the truck. After helping his grandmother and Ebony inside, Dane slid into the driver's seat. He glanced at Tatym. "If this is a dead end, we'll set a trap."

"Thank you. I'm thinking it's time for me and Ebony to come up here alone. You and I will have a public falling-out. Frank will come for me if I'm alone."

"You won't be alone. I'll be living in your attic." He turned the key in the ignition and spun gravel speeding away from her place.

"He'll see you."

"That's the only way I'll go along with this crazy scheme of yours."

"What about June? You can't leave her alone." High spots of color appeared on her cheeks.

"I'll go to my sister's house in Langley. You keep me out of this argument." June grinned. "Or better yet, save it for your public display."

"I'm pretty sure we can come up with something else to fight about." Dane took a curve too sharp and slowed, not wanting to have an accident. "Let's save this until we're out of the truck, please."

The rest of the drive to the sheriff's office was made in stony silence. His jaw was clenched so tight his teeth ached. If this was what falling for a woman was like, he needed to think twice about it. The harder he fell, the more they butted heads.

Sheriff Westbrook waited in front of the building

and motioned for them to follow him.

Dane nodded and pulled behind the sheriff's car. "Let's go find something to catch Frank with."

Chapter Twenty

Tatym peered around the two men at the video feed from the night before. "Are you sure that's Frank?" With a hat pulled low and large sunglasses, very little of the man's face showed. "It could be anybody."

"Oh, it's him." The woman behind them popped her gum. "I know Frank from way back. Didn't expect to see him here to shower, but whatever. Look—" She rewound the video further. "Before the new tee shirt and hat. Looks like he's been sleeping in his car."

A very ragged Frank purchased the hat and shirt. Tatym glanced up at Dane. "We never suspected he'd sleep in his truck."

"No, we didn't." Sheriff Westbrook shook his head. "That doesn't exactly narrow down our search."

June entered the room. "He spent last night in his truck between two semis. One of the other drivers spotted his truck."

"You know this how?" The sheriff faced her.

"By asking questions and describing Frank and the truck." She gave a sly grin. "Maybe you should deputize me."

He laughed. "If I did, everyone would quit. Good work, though." He thanked the store clerk and led them outside to where they'd parked.

"There's the driver I spoke with." June pointed to a large man eating a hot dog as he walked to his rig.

"Maybe he can tell us something more." Sheriff Westbrook led them in the man's direction.

He frowned until he spotted June. "Hey, little lady. More questions?"

"The sheriff has a few." She smiled. "Now, play nice."

He gave an exaggerated sigh. "This about the man sleeping in his truck? What'd he do?"

"Murder suspect and stalker."

Tatym's eyes widened. Having the sheriff say those words to a complete stranger set her back. Maybe the contract and Frank's son's missing insulin were the last things needed to pin the crime securely on him.

"He stalking one of these ladies?"

The sheriff nodded.

"I don't cotton to a man harassing a woman. Your suspect left at first light. Pulled out slow without turning on his lights. That made me suspicious. I wrote down his license plate if you want." Finished with his hot dog, he wiped his hands on his jeans.

"We have it, thanks. Is the driver from the other truck here?"

"No. He had a cross-country trip to make. I can't tell you more, and I'm headed out myself. Sally Mae inside will keep a lookout for you. If I see him on the road, I'll give you a call."

"Thank you." The sheriff handed him a business card.

All they'd managed to do was confirm Frank had spent the night at the truck stop. They were no closer to finding him than they were earlier. "Now what?"

"I'm calling in a helicopter." Sheriff Westbrook opened his car door. "We'll search every road in a thirty-mile radius, and we'll get a better look from the sky. As for the three of you, be careful."

"We're formulating a trap." June studied her nails.

The sheriff narrowed his eyes. "A what?"

"A trap." She grinned. "To lure Frank out of hiding. Our dear Tatym is the bait. Don't worry. It'll be safe. Dane will be around."

His eyes darted from June to Tatym to Dane. "I thought you were smarter than this."

"Outnumbered." A muscle ticked in Dane's jaw. "My grandmother is leaving town. Tatym and I will be at the cabin where I'll stay out of sight. Oh, after we have a public fight to explain why we'll no longer be joined at the hip."

It did sound foolish spoken out loud, she thought. "Do you have a better idea?"

"Yeah. Let me handle this before you get yourselves killed." He got in his car and slammed the door before rolling down the window. "If I find out you're doing something stupid, I'll lock all three of you behind bars for your own protection." He sped away.

"That didn't go well." Tatym hurried to Dane's truck. "We can figure out how to trap Frank over lunch. I'm starving. How does a pizza sound?"

"Didn't the sheriff's threat mean anything?" Dane opened the door for her.

"Only that we need to be careful not to get killed or arrested." She tossed him a grin and slid into the truck.

"Buckle up." June patted him on his good shoulder. "Between the three of us, we'll come up with a foolproof plan. Wait and see."

"You're still leaving town." Dane closed the door after his grandmother and winced at the force he'd used.

They arrived at the local pizza place shortly after noon. Almost every booth in the place was packed. Talking without being overheard might be difficult. Nope. The place was so noisy no one could hear the other tables. Good. She'd do whatever it took to catch Frank and move on with her life. Shoulders squared, she walked ahead of Dane and June. "Three," she told the hostess.

The woman led them to a middle booth by the window. "Your server will be here in a minute."

"What time are you supposed to be at your sister's?" Dane picked up a menu. "Ya'll want to share or order separately?"

"I didn't say, and why not order one large mega meat?"

"Sounds good to me." Tatym slid her menu to the edge of the table.

"Then, we'll take you after lunch."

"I'm not packed."

Dane peered up from his menu. "So, pack. I'm ordering a side of wings."

June folded her arms. "Are you going to be grumpy until that man is found?"

"I'm going to be grumpy until the two of you come to your senses without forcing me to do something that's going to end badly."

"I'm going to the restroom. Try to be in a better mood when I return." June marched to the other side of the restaurant.

"It'll be fine. We'll be expecting him. Being caught

unawares is what's dangerous. You should know that firsthand." Tatym tilted her head.

"Why do you think I'm so against you facing him?" He rubbed his shoulder.

Tatym reached across the table and rested her hand over his. "We're going to be very careful."

~

Look at them eating pizza as if they hadn't ruined his life. Frank slowed as he passed the pizza place. Imagine his surprise at seeing Dane's truck stop at the curb and the very ones he sought pile out. The sling on the man's arm filled him with glee.

He passed and turned the corner for another glimpse of them. Maybe, if the opportunity presented itself, he'd do more than just look.

Having traded his truck for a plain white one he'd had in the garage waiting for his construction logo to be added to the doors, he felt safe cruising around the block. Another white truck with another Razorback fan driving through town wouldn't warrant a second glance from those on the sidewalk.

He slowed again and chuckled as Tatym leaned across the table to lay her hand on Dane's. Grabbing the automatic rifle from the passenger seat, he raised the weapon and sprayed the window with bullets.

~

Tatym had straightened in her seat as the window shattered. Without a second thought, Dane dove across the table and tackled her to the floor. As screams filled the air and bullets flew, he searched the room for his grandmother.

It didn't seem as if she'd left the restroom yet. Hopefully, that meant she was out of the line of fire.

Within seconds, the gunfire ceased. Dane sprang to his feet, ignoring the searing pain in his shoulder. "Anyone see the shooter?"

A man holding a hand to his bleeding shoulder nodded. "White man driving a white truck wearing a Razorback hat."

Frank.

Dane helped Tatym to her feet. "Are you hurt?"

"No, but others here weren't so lucky." She pulled her cell phone from her pocket. "The screen is shattered."

Spotting all the phones to ears, Dane suspected the sheriff's department would receive plenty of calls. He held up his badge and headed for the front door. "No one leave until you're cleared."

Dane cast another look toward the women's restroom. He breathed a sigh of relief to see his grandmother supporting another woman. Now focused on his job as a deputy, he moved around the room assessing casualties. No one had died, a few injuries, nothing that couldn't be repaired. It could have been a lot worse.

Sirens wailed in the distance. Help was coming. Dane turned as Tatym came to his side. "Frank intended to shoot you." He wrapped his good arm around her. "If you hadn't sat back when you did…"

She sagged against him. "That thought occurred to me, too. I've decided not to set a trap. Frank will come on his own."

Unfortunately, true. Which meant they'd be virtual prisoners in the house. "I think we should still go through with sending my grandmother away and moving to the cabin. There are a lot of places for him to hide in the trees, but we still have more vantage points to see him coming than here in town."

Her heart beat against the palm of his hand. "I'm sorry for being obstinate. You were right all along."

"Not a coward?" He gave a lopsided smile.

"Those words never came from my mouth." Her arms snaked around him. "Nor would they ever."

When the sheriff and a deputy pulled up outside, an ambulance right behind them, Dane stepped back. "I'll have to go speak with them."

Her gaze softened. "I know. I'll see where I'm needed here."

Sadly, they both knew the drill after Wilbur's truck crashed through the window of Lucy's Diner. Help the paramedics by finding out who was injured and how. Not a tough task since those who'd been shot clustered together.

Others had been cut by flying glass. One man had a piece of wood from the hostess desk embedded in his leg. A toddler wailed in his mother's arms. Again, he reminded himself no one had died. This time.

"Pretty sure it was Frank from the description," he told the sheriff as he removed the sling from his arm.

"Ready to come off?"

"Doctor didn't say, but I'm going to need both arms. The man on the floor there saw the shooter, by the way."

He nodded. "Witnesses outside gave descriptions that matched Frank. No one had paid any attention until the gunfire." His eyes flashed. "How is he moving around right under our noses?"

"We think Tatym was the target. Frank also used an automatic rifle. He's willing to kill other people in order to get to her." Dane's hands curled into fists. He envisioned them wrapped around the man's meaty neck.

"I see the worry in your eyes." The sheriff clapped him on the shoulder. "I went through something similar with my wife. Be vigilant. Hide Tatym. Don't let her out of your sight."

"I don't intend to. We're heading up the mountain after dropping off my grandmother. There is no trap. He'll come."

"You taking Tatym up there is a trap for you more than him."

"We'll see him coming." He glanced to where Tatym offered the crying toddler a slice of pizza crust. "Up there, he can't hurt innocent people."

"I don't have the manpower to check on you more than twice a day. I'll send them at irregular intervals so Frank doesn't get used to the schedule. Why won't the two of you go with June?"

"If he finds us, my grandmother and her sister will be in danger. The way it is now, it's me and Tatym. No one else."

The sheriff didn't look convinced. "Let's hope there aren't three dead bodies when this is all over."

Chapter Twenty-One

Frank listened to the local news channel on his truck's radio. There had been no deaths from the shooting at the pizza parlor which made his heart glad. He really didn't want to harm anyone but Tatym. And Dane if he got in the way.

Shooting up the pizza place had been a rash move on his part. Yet, it felt strangely satisfying to pull that trigger.

Becky would be heartbroken to hear him named as the suspect. His boys wouldn't understand. Frank had dug himself a hole too deep to climb out of. Now, he had to make his sacrifice worth it all. He wouldn't stick around afterward to cause his family more embarrassment.

His funds would soon run out. He did have some more stashed at the construction site. Time to retrieve what was there. Sure, he had quite a lot in the bank, but Becky would need that. Best he take what lay around, finish off Tatym, letting her know exactly why he was ridding the world of the last Billings, and skip off to Mexico. He could live a simple life there, even start a new business with a new name.

Satisfied he had a foolproof plan, he headed to the

construction site. No one other than the security guard would be there, and he wouldn't be difficult to dispose of.

~

Rocking on the front porch next to Dane felt natural, even comforting, despite the danger lurking out there. She cut him a sideways glance, picturing them as an old couple. They'd rock and talk and laugh. Every morning they'd watch the sun dispel the mist over the valley. It all seemed idyllic to her.

Two things stood between her and the dream. Frank and the fact she had no idea how Dane felt about her. Kissing was one thing, love something else. Tatym loved him. She'd do anything to keep him safe, even stay at the cabin where she'd eventually confront Frank. Which meant she needed a way to send Dane back to town.

Dane, who had been sleeping, opened his eyes and smiled. "How about a field trip? A clandestine one."

"Oh?"

"Let's snoop around the construction office. I'll think up something to satisfy Roy by the time we arrive. My gut tells me there's something there that might give us a lead as to where Frank is headed." He reached out his hand. "Well?"

She'd go anywhere with him. "Sounds like an exciting night." Especially since Frank would be an idiot to be at his office. "Won't the sheriff have someone watching the place?"

"You saw how big the grounds were. It'll be easy to sneak in from one of the sides, and that's provided there's someone in front of the property and someone else behind." He stood, pulling her to her feet.

"Let me put on some gym shoes, and I'll be right

out." She slipped her hand free and hurried to her room.

Dane was right. Next to his house, the office was where Frank would keep anything important. Since nothing had been found at his home, they might get lucky at his work.

Dressed in more comfortable shoes, baggy shorts, and an oversize top, she might not be fashionable, but she could move easily—an added bonus of not having to worry about getting good clothes dirty. Her eyes widened at the sight of Ebony. "We're taking the dog?"

"Best warning system around. She can watch our backs." He tapped the side of the truck. "Let's go."

A cloudy sky provided plenty of shadows to give them cover. Dane parked his truck down the street where several other vehicles sat.

"Stay close." He pulled a flashlight from the glove compartment.

"Like glue." She slid from the truck and scanned the area. In an older part of town with few residences—mostly mobile homes—no one was out. A few lights burned in windows, a dog barked at their presence, but all seemed quiet otherwise.

Tatym followed so close behind Dane she could smell his aftershave. Brisk, clean, and so like him. She breathed in deep. This would all be over soon, and he'd go his way. She might as well enjoy him while she could.

He held his hand up, and she almost bumped into him. She counted to five before he motioned her forward.

Tatym glanced at Ebony. The dog's hair wasn't raised, and she trotted, tongue lolling, beside them.

Once they reached the side of the property, they climbed over an iron gate hung high enough Ebony could squeeze under. Tatym froze halfway as the heavy chain holding the gate closed jangled. When no other noise reached her ears, she jumped down.

Dane caught her with ease. "You don't weigh more than a minute."

"So, I've heard my whole life." She'd always been petite. It no longer bothered her when she was carded at the store. As long as Dane didn't treat her like a child, everything was good.

The beam from the flashlight lit up the path in front of them. They stayed behind stacks of trusses and two-by-fours as much as possible.

The building sat black. Not like the last time they'd been here when a light had glowed from a window.

"Where's the security guard?" She clutched the back of Dane's shirt.

"I don't know. Something doesn't feel right."

Ebony whined, then growled, her dark eyes fixated on the building.

Goose bumps prickled Tatym's skin. Were they going to confront Frank here? "Did you bring your gun?" She whispered.

"Yes."

She felt it now. Her fingers rested on the barrel of the weapon at his back. If Dane couldn't reach it in time, she could.

~

They were here. Frank grinned and backed away from the window.

Things would end tonight, but first he wanted to play. He set the radio in his office to a station that played acid rock, placed it in the office doorway, and cranked the volume to its highest setting. While he knew the layout of the building, the other two didn't. Now, they'd hear less than they could see. He slipped on the infrared headpiece.

~

Dane's blood ran cold as the music blasted. They'd never be able to hear Frank coming, and he had no doubt Grayson was in the building.

With Tatym gripping his shirt and Ebony pressed close his leg, the three inched across the concrete floor of the warehouse section of Grayson's Construction.

The bass of the music pounded in his head. His hand holding the flashlight started to sweat. Dane's heart threatened to burst through his ribcage. If Tatym wasn't here with him, the anxiety would be less. His wanting to snoop might be the last of both of them. He sent a quick prayer for protection to heaven.

A shot rang out. The bullet knocked the flashlight out of his hand and shattered the bulb. They were cast into total darkness with the music still blaring.

Was Frank that good of a shot, or had knocking the flashlight out of Dane's hand been sheer luck?

The hand at his back trembled. "I can't see anything."

"Neither can I. We'll have to rely on Ebony's body language."

"I can't see her body."

"But you can feel her." He placed his hand on Ebony's head. The dog trembled as much as Tatym did. How well could Ebony hear over the music? He leaned over to speak to the dog. "Go."

Ebony jetted forward, then stopped.

Dane no longer felt Tatym's hand on him. His heart skipped a beat. "Tatym?" When he received no response, he told Ebony to find her.

The dog whined and moved slowly enough Dane had no trouble keeping his hand on her head.

"Ow. My foot."

Dane frowned. "You let go."

"I tripped over something. I'm holding onto Ebony's tail now."

Dane dropped to his knees. "Don't move. I'll see what it is and clear the path." If he could find it. He crawled in a six-foot circle.

His hands landed on something soft—a face—one that didn't react. "Pretty sure you tripped over the security guard." He patted down to the man's neck, then came into contact with blood over his chest. Dane had no doubt the man was dead. Rising to his feet, he inched the short distance until he ran into Tatym and the dog.

"A dead body?" Tatym shuddered.

Something tapped his right shoulder. "Did you just touch me?" he whispered.

"No."

A harder tap with something hard, then nothing. Frank was playing them, and he could see in the dark.

Dane reached forward until he could touch Tatym, then gripped her arm and yanked her close. He hated being rough, but their lives were on the line, and he wanted her so close to his side a hot flame would meld them together. "Ebony, come."

He knew Frank could see them, but they needed a place he'd have to work to reach them. Dane's hand brushed a pile of wood, then another, and another like a maze of some sort. He ducked behind one. "If we keep our backs together and Ebony close, we might sense him coming." Right. Like he had the tap on his shoulder. At least they were no longer in the middle of a cavernous room.

The music ended abruptly. The silence drummed in Dane's ears. After several minutes, no sound came at all except the low-throated whine of the dog.

With his back pressed against Tatym's, he felt like he should have a sword in his hand. He reached behind him and gripped his gun, slowly pulling it free, then eased off the safety. If anyone came in front of him, he'd shoot as long as Tatym stayed at his back. His ears strained to hear more than Tatym's ragged breathing. God, don't let Frank hear her. Don't let Ebony bark.

His heart lodged in his throat as a scuffle sounded on the other side of the wood. Footsteps that paused, then moved on. Dare Dane risk his cell phone? He slipped his free hand into the back pocket of his jeans.

The screen lit up as he placed a quick text to the sheriff. Hopefully, the man would hear an alert that one came through. It being after eleven p.m., the sheriff was most likely asleep.

He quickly turned the screen off. No sound came to let him know whether or not their location had been discovered. How long did they have until Frank found them? Dare he risk their lives by moving? Think, man. His eyes had adjusted to the outline of the wood in front of him. The clouds parted a bit filling the room with a silver glow. Dane peered around the pile in front of him.

Frank stood in the center of an open space and turned in a slow circle, night-vision goggles in one hand. "It's only a matter of time before I find you. If you're tired of our game of hide-n-seek, you can come out. I'll end it here for you, Mr. Temporary Deputy, but I still need the gal."

No way would Dane turn over Tatym. Not a chance.

He raised his gun, then lowered it. He couldn't be assured of a hit at this distance.

The dog growled low in her throat. Tatym patted her head. "No," she whispered.

Dane motioned for them to move slowly backward. The more distance between them and the other man the better.

A cloud obscured the moon again. Another minute to waste while his eyes adjusted to the dark, then Dane kept backing up deeper and deeper into the spaces between stacks of plywood. Further on lay bags of concrete. Eventually, they'd literally be backed against a wall.

Frank would find them, and either he or Dane would be dead.

Chapter Twenty-two

Piles of construction supplies were pressing in on her. Tatym's heart beat in her ears so loudly she almost wished for the blaring music to play again. If not for the company of Dane and Ebony, she'd have given herself away out of sheer fear. She gripped the back of Dane's shirt so tightly her knuckles ached. Her other hand gripped the dog's tail. When Dane stopped, she stumbled into the back of him, her nose pressed flat.

"I see light," Dane whispered.

She peered around him. The light appeared to be coming from a tunnel. Offices, perhaps? "Should we make a run for it?"

"I'm thinking it's a trap. A building this huge must have a side door. That's what we need to find."

She couldn't see over the piles much less more than inches in front of her. Dane would have to find the exit. He'd never failed to find a way before.

Hope leaped within her as he took a decisive step forward, then another and another until the clouds parted again and the moon showed the way. A door was indeed on the side wall. All they had to do was sprint to it without being shot. What was Dane waiting for?

The moon disappeared again.

"Run."

Their feet pounded the concrete as Dane led them from cover into the open. Tatym couldn't see a thing and prayed Dane had found a clear path.

Sirens wailed outside.

"This isn't the last we'll meet," Frank yelled from their left. "Next time, I won't be playing."

Dane slammed against a locked door. "We'll have to go out the way we came in. It'll be fine. Frank is leaving."

Echoing footsteps proved he ran toward the light they'd spotted.

"He's escaping." She stopped. "We have to go after him. We're on the offensive now. Come on." Despite his warning, she darted forward, using the light to guide her.

"Stop, Tatym." Dane thundered after her, grabbing her by the shoulder and whipping her around to face him. "You'd be running into a trap. Let the sheriff handle this. Frank can't go far."

"Yes, he can." She yanked away. "We have to catch him," her voice pleaded.

"That's all right." Gun in hand, Frank stepped from the light. "Tatym is going to go with me, or I shoot you and the dog."

Dane made a move to step in front of her.

Ebony barked, the noise echoing off the concrete walls.

"You have until the first deputy steps through that door, then he dies, too." Frank tilted his head.

Tatym stood on tiptoe; her lips close to Dane's ear. "Come save me." She planted a tender kiss on his cheek and moved to Frank's side.

"Tatym, no." Dane's voice cracked. "Where are you

taking her?"

"The last place you'd expect. Adios. Come after us, and I'll kill you. I've nothing to lose now." Frank took her arm and started to run.

"There's no need to strong-arm me. I came willingly." She tried to swallow past a dry throat. How long until he tried to kill her? Did she have minutes, hours, days before she no longer lived?

"I'll drop you here if the law reaches us before we can flee." He shoved her toward a steel door at the end of a hallway. "This place is a labyrinth for those unfamiliar."

"You had this planned, didn't you?"

"Always prepared." He punched some numbers into a keypad on the wall, then shoved the door open.

They stepped into another hall, this one only lit by nightlights. Frank slammed the door behind them. This tunnel led outside where Tatym squeezed between a large bush with spiky leaves and the warm concrete building.

"Keep going."

"These hurt."

"They make the perfect deterrent, don't they?"

Actually, they did. She lunged from them almost hitting her head on the bed of a dark-colored truck. This man must have a garage to choose from the way he kept changing vehicles. Without being told, she climbed into the passenger seat as Frank did the driver's. Her time to try and escape would come, but it had to be when Dane wasn't in danger by being close.

She'd told him to find her, but that was the last thing she wanted. Unless, she could walk into his arms. No, she wouldn't risk him. Not even to save her own life.

Frank sped down a narrow asphalt road, through some trees, and out onto a highway. No lights flashed behind them. He'd managed to evade the sheriff again.

She took a deep breath, ignoring her seatbelt. If she found the opportunity to dive out of the truck she would. No, he'd shoot her in the back. Her hand hovered near the handle.

"Don't be an idiot." Frank laughed. "If you would have given me what I wanted, this could have been avoided."

"It isn't yours."

"It should've been." Spittle flew from his lips. "My grandfather told me so. He told me the deed your grandmother had was fake."

"You were lied to." Tatym had heard the gossip about her great grandfather and a local rival. She'd only paid half attention when her grandmother would speak of it, but hopefully she knew enough to pierce Frank's insanity. "Did you ever hear how my family acquired the land? I'm talking right after the Civil War."

"Might as well tell me. We have another twenty minutes before we reach the cabin."

He was taking her home? "One man by the name of Hayes bet this land in a poker game and lost. My ancestor won it in a poker game. The Billings family has been feuding with the Hayes ever since." She remembered more than she thought she would.

"So, it is mine. Hayes is my mother's family name."

"No, your man lost."

He smirked. "The right man won't lose this time." He careened around a hairpin curve. "Isn't it right that I end this at the overlook? That land is the center of the trouble, after all."

Now, she had options. Barricade herself in the cabin if she could reach it in time, or make a dash for the trees. Both were risky as bullets moved a lot faster than she did.

~

Dane pounded his fist against his thigh. Did Tatym sacrifice herself to spare his life? Absolutely no way. He gave chase, skidding to a halt as a door slammed before he could reach it.

He stared at the keypad. No way in without the code. He raced back down the hall, meeting up with Sheriff Westbrook and a deputy. "That way is locked. There has to be another way out of here."

"We haven't seen anything. There are men walking the perimeter."

"I doubt Frank is holing up behind that locked door. He'll have provided a way out." Dane sprinted around the building, the sheriff and Ebony on his heels. "Find Tatym, girl."

The dog bolted ahead, stopping near a large bush. She glanced at Dane and barked.

He parted the bush's branches, receiving a few scratches in the process. A door, left open about an inch, had been hidden by the foliage. "They're gone." His heart sank.

"What did Frank say when he took her?"

"That he'd take her where I'd least suspect." Dane widened his eyes. "The cabin."

"Makes sense to me. Let's go. I'll drive."

"Come, Ebony." All he could do was pray they'd reach Tatym in time.

The sheriff sped from the scene, siren and lights clearing the road in front of them. Not that many were out this late at night. Which meant Frank had a clear path, too.

~

"Now what?" Tatym stood in the middle of her yard.

"You jump." Frank gave her an evil grin. "I've watched you most mornings stand here, cup in hand, and watch the sun rise. I want you to jump and watch the mist fade away when you hit bottom. Or—" his grin widened, "you give me the deed."

She frowned. "Why? It would be worthless without a bill of sale."

"I'm talking about the authentic deed." He took a step toward her. "The one Dane received at the diner."

"That's the fake one." She found herself being inched toward the cliff. "We had it made to force you to come out of hiding. If you want to see it, it's in the cabin. I'll show you."

"I'll find it once you're over the edge. We don't have a lot of time. Dane is bound to know I meant this place as the last he'd suspect. They consider me an idiot, but I'm planning on being gone before they arrive. Now, either you jump or I shoot you and throw you over. On the count of three, shall we? One… Two…"

Tatym jumped, grabbing for trees' branches on her way. Too far for her to reach the edge, she stopped at an oak tree, the breath knocked from her lungs as she hung over a thick branch. She coughed and gasped at the pain in her side.

Glancing down she saw a stick protruding from her side. She couldn't stay pinned like a bug in a display case. Before she could change her mind, she pulled the stick free. Her scream startled roosting birds from the trees.

It took a bit of effort, but she managed to rip off part of the oversized shirt she wore and bind the wound. Tatym gasped for air, trying to figure out how to get out of the tree without falling further. She could use the trees, inching from one to the other until she reached the rock face. A narrow ledge would give her a place to rest and figure out how to reach the top. She winced and grabbed for a branch, feeling a bit like a flying squirrel.

Please, God, don't let me fall.

Her foot slipped as she reached for another branch. She took a slight leap, landing on the branch of a maple tree. Not as steady as the oak but so far so good.

A shot rang out from the top of the cliff. She hoped Dane hadn't come after her alone.

Chapter Twenty-Three

Dane ducked behind the passenger door of Sheriff Westbrook's car as Frank fired at them. He scanned the yard. Where was she?

"Where is Tatym Billings?" The sheriff called out.

"Over the cliff." Frank laughed and fired again from the protection of the porch.

Dane's heart stopped. He had to go to her. See if she had fallen all the way. His throat clogged at the thought he'd never see her again. Her body might never be found.

This land would go up for sale, just as Frank wanted. Except, the man would be in prison for the rest of his life, and a stranger would purchase Tatym's favorite place. No. He wouldn't let that happen. Dane would pay any price to stay where the woman he loved had last been.

Anger roiled through him, and he stood. He grabbed the extra weapon the sheriff had set on the seat and, with a gun in both hands like a gunfighter from an old western, he marched forward, firing one gun after the other.

His shots went wild, but they were enough to keep Frank hunkered down.

"You're the craziest man I've ever met." The sheriff stepped beside him.

"Blind rage will do that to a man." His words came cold and hard from a tortured throat. "I'm sure you can relate. Everyone in town knows the story of how you met your wife."

"True." They stood over a defiant Frank.

"You're under arrest for the murder of Alice Billings and the kidnapping and alleged murder of Tatym Billings. Put down the gun." The sheriff kept his gun trained on the other man.

Ebony set off a frenzy of barking and raced for the cliff's ledge.

Dane shot the sheriff a look of shock and took off after the dog. "Tatym!"

"Dane? I'm here."

He peered over the edge to see her straddling a thick tree branch. He'd never been more relieved to see anyone in his life. "Hold on. I'll go find a rope. Are you okay?"

"Possibly some cracked ribs, but other than that, I'm fine. Unless you leave me out here much longer. I'm tired." Tears had left tracks on her dirty face, ripping at his heart.

"Not much longer."

"Watch out." The sheriff took aim at the back of a fleeing Frank.

Frank sprinted for the cliff's edge, his hardened gaze fixated on Dane.

"Shoot him," Dane yelled.

"Never shot a man in the back before and won't start now."

Dane had never shot a man, period, but he didn't hesitate to aim and fire.

His shot sent Frank careening over the edge.

Ebony's barks threatened to make Dane's ears

bleed.

He watched in horror as he bounced off the ledge Tatym sat on, dislodging her. His body continued to bounce down the cliffside, but now Tatym hung, only her hands grasping a branch. "Get me a rope, Sheriff. Tatym's down here."

Seconds later he held a strong nylon cord in his hands. He recognized it as one of the supplies he'd left to rebuild the garage. He tied one end into a loop.

"You'll have to put this around your waist, sweetheart. Try to back on to that branch." Please, don't fall.

"I can't." Her face paled under the dirt.

"Sheriff, you'll have to lower me. Use the dog." Dane slipped the loop around his waist.

Sheriff Westbrook nodded. "We'll pull you up." He tied the rope around the dog's neck, then around his waist. Good. Between the two, man and dog, they ought to be able to bring up him and Tatym.

He turned around and rappelled down the cliff, trusting the sheriff to hold him. Dane had no other choice but to trust. Saving Tatym was his only priority. He'd die if he had to.

Navigating trees, saplings, and bushes wasn't an easy task. It was a miracle Tatym was in one piece since Dane's shirt now bore several holes, and scratches marred his arms. "I'm coming."

"Hurry. I can't feel my fingers."

Far too long before he stood even with her. "I need you to wrap your arms around my neck, then ease onto my back like a monkey."

"Who is pulling us up?"

"The sheriff and Ebony."

She shook her head. "No, you go. We'll be too heavy."

He laughed. "Darlin', you're the tiniest woman I've ever met. They can manage both of us. Your hundred and ten pounds isn't enough to make us too heavy."

She narrowed her eyes, using her legs to help move her closer to him. "How do you know how much I weigh?"

"I'm used to eyeing horses." He snaked his arm around her waist and pulled her close. His wounded shoulder screamed. Her weight was a lot for a not-yet-healed shoulder. "Hold on. Okay, pull us up."

Tatym's arms tightened around his neck.

"You're choking me."

"Sorry." She pressed her head against his back. "Thank you for coming for me."

He sniffed back tears. "When Frank said you went over the cliff, I thought I'd lost you."

"Me too. I wish he could have been saved rather than go over."

A sharp pain pierced Dane's heart. "I had to shoot him. He planned on taking me over with him."

"Which means you couldn't have saved me."

At the top, the sheriff smiled down at them, stretching out his hand. "Let's get you two on solid ground."

With a solid grip, and Dane walking up the cliff face, the sheriff managed to lift Tatym to safety. He stood her on her feet and ran his hands up and down her, assessing for damage.

"I'm fine. Really." She cupped his face. "Just the ribs, which your touching doesn't help." Her lips curled into a smile. "Thank you again."

Sheriff Westbrook cleared his throat and headed toward his car. "Y'all let me know when you're ready to go into town."

Dane chuckled, pressing his forehead against Tatym's. "I've never been more frightened in my life."

"Imagine how I felt. He kept threatening to kill you."

"After you, I guess."

She shrugged. "He made me jump. I aimed for the nearest tree."

"You really are a little monkey."

"Don't even start." She laughed. "I love you, Dane James. I can't remember the moment I started loving you. It seems as if my heart simply waited for you to come into my life."

Warmth rushed through him as he tilted her face to his. "I love you, too. While I want life with you to be an adventure, can it be a bit tamer?"

She tilted her head. "Are you asking me to marry you? Here? Right after we both almost died?"

"I am. Will you marry me, Tatym Billings? Will you watch the sun push away the mist each morning while I kiss you?"

"For the rest of my life. Now kiss me."

He was more than happy to oblige.

The End

Don't miss the next book, Bitter Isolation

Dear Reader,

I hope you're enjoying the adventures of the residents in Misty Hollow. If you've enjoyed Lethal Inheritance, please go to Amazon and leave a review. Reviews are the lifeblood of an author. Also please sign up for my newsletter and follow me on social media to keep up with any of my writing news.

Cynthia Hickey

Connect with me on
FaceBook
Twitter
Sign up for my newsletter and receive a free short story
www.cynthiahickey.com
Follow me on
Amazon
Bookbub

Enjoy other books by Cynthia Hickey

Misty Hollow
Secrets of Misty Hollow
Deceptive Peace
Calm Surface
Lightning Never Strikes Twice

The Tail Waggin' Mysteries
Cat-Eyed Witness
The Dog Who Found a Body
Troublesome Twosome
Four-Legged Suspect
Unwanted Christmas Guest
Wedding Day Cat Burglar

Brothers Steele
Sharp as Steele
Carved in Steele
Forged in Steele
Brothers Steele (All three in one)

The Brothers of Copper Pass
Wyatt's Warrant
Dirk's Defense
Stetson's Secret
Houston's Hope
Dallas's Dare

Kodak Kill Shot, book 4
To Snap a Killer
Hollywood Murder Mysteries

Shady Acres Mysteries
Beware the Orchids, book 1
Path to Nowhere
Poison Foliage
Poinsettia Madness
Deadly Greenhouse Gases
Vine Entrapment
Shady Acres Boxed Set

CLEAN BUT GRITTY Romantic Suspense

Highland Springs

Murder Live
Say Bye to Mommy
To Breathe Again
Highland Springs Murders (all 3 in one)

Colors of Evil Series

Shades of Crimson
Coral Shadows

The Pretty Must Die Series

Ripped in Red, book 1

Pierced in Pink, book 2
Wounded in White, book 3
Worthy, The Complete Story

Lisa Paxton Mystery Series

Eenie Meenie Miny Mo
Jack Be Nimble
Hickory Dickory Dock
Boxed Set

Hearts of Courage
A Heart of Valor
The Game
Suspicious Minds
After the Storm
Local Betrayal
Hearts of Courage Boxed Set

Overcoming Evil series
Mistaken Assassin
Captured Innocence
Mountain of Fear
Exposure at Sea
A Secret to Die for
Collision Course
Romantic Suspense of 5 books in 1

INSPIRATIONAL

Nosy Neighbor Series
Anything For A Mystery, Book 1
A Killer Plot, Book 2
Skin Care Can Be Murder, Book 3
Death By Baking, Book 4
Jogging Is Bad For Your Health, Book 5
Poison Bubbles, Book 6
A Good Party Can Kill You, Book 7
Nosy Neighbor collection

Christmas with Stormi Nelson

The Summer Meadows Series
Fudge-Laced Felonies, Book 1
Candy-Coated Secrets, Book 2
Chocolate-Covered Crime, Book 3
Maui Macadamia Madness, Book 4
All four novels in one collection

The River Valley Mystery Series
Deadly Neighbors, Book 1
Advance Notice, Book 2
The Librarian's Last Chapter, Book 3
All three novels in one collection

Historical cozy
Hazel's Quest

Historical Romances
Runaway Sue
Taming the Sheriff
Sweet Apple Blossom
A Doctor's Agreement
A Lady Maid's Honor
A Touch of Sugar
Love Over Par
Heart of the Emerald
A Sketch of Gold
Her Lonely Heart

Finding Love the Harvey Girl Way
Cooking With Love
Guiding With Love
Serving With Love
Warring With Love
All 4 in 1

Finding Love in Disaster
The Rancher's Dilemma
The Teacher's Rescue
The Soldier's Redemption

Woman of courage Series

A Love For Delicious
Ruth's Redemption

Charity's Gold Rush
Mountain Redemption
They Call Her Mrs. Sheriff
Woman of Courage series

Short Story Westerns
Desert Rose
Desert Lilly
Desert Belle
Desert Daisy
Flowers of the Desert 4 in 1

Contemporary

Romance in Paradise
Maui Magic
Sunset Kisses
Deep Sea Love
3 in 1

Finding a Way Home
Service of Love
Hillbilly Cinderella
Unraveling Love
I'd Rather Kiss My Horse

Christmas
Dear Jillian
Romancing the Fabulous Cooper Brothers
Handcarved Christmas

The Payback Bride
Curtain Calls and Christmas Wishes
Christmas Gold
A Christmas Stamp
Snowflake Kisses
Merry's Secret Santa
A Christmas Deception

The Red Hat's Club (Contemporary novellas)

Finally
Suddenly
Surprisingly
The Red Hat's Club 3 – in 1

Short Story

One Hour (A short story thriller)
Whisper Sweet Nothings (a Valentine short romance)